The moon came out full again, and Steve risked a quick glimpse through one of the glassless windows. He almost choked in rage. Linda was bound to one of the supporting posts, and while he couldn't plainly see her face, he thought a cloth was tied around her mouth.

He stared briefly at her, his eyes burning. Steve had never known such a killing rage . . .

Also by Giles A. Lutz
Published by Ballantine Books:

LURE OF THE OUTLAW TRAIL

THE TRESPASSERS

THE ECHO

FORT APACHE

FORKED TONGUE

KILLER'S TRAIL

Giles A. Lutz

BALLANTINE BOOKS • NEW YORK

Copyright © 1980 by Giles A. Lutz

All rights reserved. Published in the United States by Ballantine Books, a division of Random House, Inc., New York, and simultaneously in Canada by Random House of Canada, Limited, Toronto, Canada.

Library of Congress Catalog Card Number: 79-8704

ISBN 0-345-29441-6

This edition published by arrangement with Doubleday & Co., Inc.

Printed in Canada

First Ballantine Books Edition: August 1981

CHAPTER 1

Six months had passed since the Army had stepped aside and let the impatiently waiting people into Oklahoma. Great throngs had crowded the borderlines in all directions, held back by armed troopers. No one could enter the territory until noon of April 22, 1889, and at that magic hour all restraints had been removed. Everybody was given a chance of grabbing a piece of land; all the seeker had had to do was stake out his claim, then be prepared to defend his choice against all latecomers. Many an original claimer had lost his ground, however, either by guile or force.

Many a change had occurred in this country since noon of that fateful day. Towns sprang into life almost overnight, and where yesterday only vast expanses of empty prairie greeted the eye, now the land was spotted with towns of all sizes and descriptions.

Still people came, daily swelling the growth of the towns. America was land hungry, and the ads described this land as a paradise. When a man planted anything, he had better spring to one side to avoid being knocked off his feet by the quick-growing plants. The government's advertising of Oklahoma land grants had been a huge magnet, reaching far and wide to pull in those land seekers.

Guthrie was leading in population, but Oklahoma City was rapidly gaining. Some people predicted that Oklahoma City was destined to become Oklahoma's largest city.

That could readily be, Steve Truman admitted as he sauntered down the crowded street. Every inch of land was claimed, and still more people pushed into Oklahoma City, though only God knew what all these people saw in this spot.

Steve was a tall, lanky, rawboned man with an easy gait

1

that made him appear indolent. The Oklahoma sun had browned his face and bleached the hair showing below his hat, but it hadn't toned down the sharpness of those blue-gray eyes. He was only a year over his maturity, but nature hadn't paid any attention to the calendar. Steve had reached his full growth, and his six feet, two inches in height attested to that. His shoulders were broad, his chest thick, and his arms rippled with muscles. He had been born and reared on a Missouri farm, and all those hours of hard work added to his development. He moved as fluidly as flowing water, and he looked like a placid man until he was aroused. Then his eyes darkened, turning them almost black, and his jaw jutted belligerently. He had been born with a keen eye, and hunting hundreds of squirrels and rabbits had increased that gift. That hunting skill was valuable on that hardscrabble farm in the Missouri Ozarks, for many a meal would have been meatless if it hadn't been for Steve's sharp eye. The natural skill with a rifle had flowered into an equal ability with a handgun. Two dead men attested to that skill. Those two didn't rest on his conscience, for both had been lawbreakers, and the only way to take them was to resort to a gun, for they had boasted they had no intention of being taken alive. Steve had helped them to accomplish their brag with two quick, deadly shots. Steve had earned the right to wear the badge pinned to his shirt. He wasn't particularly happy with his job, but it was better than doing nothing at all. He could survive on the meager salary paid him, but he saw no chance of advancement, for there was no way to supplant Marshal Dixon unless he was shot down by some hothead. God knew, Steve didn't want that. He had been fatherless since he was sixteen, and Dixon was close to being a father to him. Steve didn't allow himself to think of what he might have become if Dixon hadn't come along and given him a purpose. Oklahoma was filled with hordes of scum who preyed on the helpless. Steve could understand that. When a man was hungry and had no scruples, he turned to stringent measures to fill that empty, aching void.

He walked along with a seeming indifference, but he was aware of everything going on around him. He weighed and evaluated every sound and sight that came to him. He'd lost his interest in that shabby little farm after his father died. His mother had died when he was no more than a toddler, and he never really knew her. The government's ad about this new virgin land had caught his eyes, and he had determined to make a run in the hope of getting hold of a better piece of land.

He put the sixty rocky acres of farmland up for sale and cut his asking price for a quicker sale. He packed his few possessions in the old, battered wagon and hitched his two plow horses to it. They were old and on the decrepit side, and it was going to be a long, tedious ride.

Steve was appalled when he saw the number of people gathered at Kingfisher Creek. Stopping in Kingfisher, he had asked where the run would start, but received little encouragement.

One little fat man looked with amusement at Steve's outfit and spit tobacco juice in the dust before he replied. "The Army is stopping the people until the time comes to start. The starting line is at Kingfisher Creek about a mile and a quarter west of here. People have been arriving for the past two weeks. Some are just camping out until the Army lets them in. A few sooners have tried to sneak in, hoping to be at the ground they already picked before the others are allowed in. The Army's been digging out the sooners."

Steve was interested. This was the first real information he had received about the run. "What does the Army do with the sooners?"

The fat man shrugged. "They just toss them back. I guess the soldiers ain't allowed to shoot them. Might be a good idea, if they did. It seems to me like Oklahoma is getting a poor class of people. If they try to break all the rules at the start, what kind of a place will this be?"

Steve couldn't answer that. "Do I have to register someplace?"

"Naw," the fat man replied. "Just go join the others, waiting for the starting signal. Jesus, there must be ten thousand people out there already. I guess a few more won't make any difference." He looked again at Steve's wagon and team. "You planning on making the run with them?" He nodded toward the sorry team.

Steve felt his neck stiffen. "Why?" he demanded.

The fat man added another messy spot to the ground around him. "Hell, you won't get anywhere. Not with that team."

He backed hastily away from Steve's darkening eyes. "I

ain't arguing with you. You'll see what I mean when you get out to the line."

Steve turned and walked away, his shoulders a stiff, injured line.

"You'll see," the fat man shouted after him. "That poor team won't last the first hour of the run."

Steve whirled, his face indignant. He took a step, and the fat man broke into a run.

Steve's face relaxed as he saw him go. He could catch him, but what good would that do? He might pummel the man for the offensive remarks, but that could bring him more trouble than satisfaction.

He walked back to his wagon and climbed up onto the driver's seat. He shook the reins at the weary team. "Come on, Betsey, Dandy," he wheedled. "Just a little more, and we'll be there."

The wagon creaked forlornly as it started forward. The fat man hadn't been lying when he said this was a sorry outfit. Just the trip from Missouri had about taken everything out of the team. He wasn't asking a long run from the jaded animals. He would stop just a little distance the other side of the line, grabbing whatever land was available. He hoped the other people making the run would be far more particular.

His heart sank as he saw the assembled throng. The fat man was right when he said ten thousand people had gathered, waiting for the magic hour.

As far as Steve could see was row after row of eager people waiting for the Army to step away from the line. A lot of people were making the run on horseback. Those horses ranged from fine Thoroughbreds down through mules and plow horses. Even the meanest of the horses weren't as sorry as his team. His eyes roamed worriedly over the open buggies, fringed carriages, prairie schooners, farm wagons, carts and racing sulkies. There were even a few high-wheeled bicycles. Hundreds of people stood on foot, trusting to good legs and sturdy lungs to win a piece of land.

Steve groaned inwardly. Those foot runners could probably beat his team. A growing conviction was swelling within him. He had come all this distance to no avail.

He doggedly shook his head and gripped the reins. He wasn't going to drop out without making some effort.

He was in the fifth row to start the run, and his heart

pounded more furiously as he heard someone shouting off the minutes left.

"Nine," the man called. "Eight, seven—"

Steve gulped and leaned forward. He breathed as hard as though he had actually run a long distance.

"Two, one," the man yelled.

The troopers fired carbines into the air, and it sounded as though every bugle in the world was being blown.

"Hiyah," Steve yelled and slapped the reins on the old rumps.

All around him people passed him, some on foot, some in carriages, some in racing sulkies. The Thoroughbreds were in full run after a few strides. In a hundred yards, they confirmed what Steve already knew: They were all going to far outdistance him. Before the afternoon was over, they would be far out of sight.

He slapped the reins again and again on those rumps in a futile attempt to get more speed out of the horses. He didn't have a whip. It wouldn't have done any good. He couldn't beat out of horseflesh what was already gone.

Just up ahead, he saw people draw to a stop and hammer stakes into the perimeters of the land they'd chosen. Even the quick, easy land was going to be snapped up long before he reached an available site.

He stood gritting his teeth, slashing again and again with the reins. The punishment dragged a weak burst of speed from the animals. There were no roads, only bumpy, prairie ground. One of the horses stepped into a prairie dog hole and went down, a shrill scream tearing from its throat. It fell heavily against the ground, dragging its teammate with it. The wagon's momentum carried it into the two downed horses, and the thump slammed Steve from his feet. He yelled hoarsely as he flew through the air. He landed heavily on his head, and that was the last thing he knew. The light was suddenly blotted out, and he felt no pain. The unconsciousness came too quickly.

Steve had no idea of how long he was out. He came to, and the pain instantly attacked him. His head ached in great, smashing blows, his neck hurt, and he was dizzy and sick.

He must be hurt worse than he thought, for when he tried to sit up, he couldn't make it. It felt as though some great weight were pinning him down. The struggle to sit up aroused the first wave of pain, and the agony increased.

He thought the top of his head was coming off, and he sank limply back, waiting for the surcease of the horrible pain.

His vision was hazy, and he was sure he must have some broken bones. He lay there, his eyes closed while he thought about it. There were voices in the distance, and Steve was sure they came from people passing him. He didn't expect any of them to stop to help him, not with the urgency this land rush had aroused in everybody.

Steve wasn't sure how long he lay there. Under these conditions, time had a way of flattening out with no definite limits. The pounding in his head had lessened, but the aching in his body seemed to have increased. He must force himself to make the effort to get on his feet. He didn't want to, for he was sure what would hit him. Pain was a savage adversary, and when it was aroused, its attack was relentless.

He sighed and opened his eyes. He could see better now. All the fuzzy outlines had disappeared. That weight was still on him, though it didn't seem as oppressive, or maybe his strength was returning.

He swore softly at what he saw. He was pinned under the wagon, and he could understand now what had happened to him. The wagon's momentum had carried it into the downed team, and the impact had overturned it. That was what threw him out of the wagon. He had either hit his head on the ground, or the overturning wagon had struck his head. His relief didn't ease his pain, but he felt a great surge of returning confidence.

The wagon was a rickety old thing, and the overturning was enough to smash it into kindling. One of the wheels lay across Steve's chest, and it took a struggle to push it aside. God, he was weak as a kitten, for he was panting with the effort.

One of the sideboards was across his legs, and he kicked it aside. He still wasn't positive he had suffered no broken bones, but moving his arms and legs hadn't sent any sharp pains coursing through him. No, he thought he was all right. It would take the final test of standing to be sure.

He was panting hard when he struggled to his feet. His head hung low, and he had to choke back the threatened nausea. He got the spasm under control. That had been close, for he could taste the sour bile that filled his throat.

He stood motionless until the weakness passed, then

looked at his team. God, what a mess. One of the horses was dead. The wagon tongue had driven into its belly, and it must have died hard, for the marks of its struggles had scored the ground around it.

Steve looked at the dead animal with pained eyes. He had spent a lot of time with old Betsey, and she had been a faithful worker in far better days.

He didn't know how long he was locked in those memories. A soft whinny of pain aroused him, and he looked at the other horse. Dandy had started this mess by stepping into a prairie dog hole.

The horse lay on its side. Every now and then, a convulsive shudder ran through him as he tried to garner enough strength to rise. All he could do was raise his head. He could get no farther, and the effort thoroughly drained him, for the head flopped back onto the ground. Steve saw the reason why he couldn't rise. The off foreleg was snapped off just about the fetlock. The white of the broken bone showed through, and only the hide had prevented the leg from coming off.

There was only one thing to do, and Steve pulled the pistol from its holster. His hand wasn't quite steady as he placed the muzzle only a few inches from Dandy's head. Those great, soft eyes were swimming in pain, and that helped Steve pull the trigger.

The blast sounded inordinately loud. The horse's head rose high, then flopped back. A grimace crossed Steve's face. This had been an ill-fated trip from its inception. He shook his head, his expression Stoic. He hoped Dandy and Betsey had gone to a better place. At least they were out of the wracking agony of old age.

Steve slipped the pistol back into the holster and tried a tentative step. His legs were sore from the bruising, but he could move them. He didn't know this country, he didn't have the slightest idea where to go.

He saw nobody near him. He looked around for his rifle, and for an instant, didn't see it. It had been leaning on the seat before the wagon crashed into the horses. The momentum of the impact must have whipped the rifle out of the wagon. He finally saw it and walked over to where it lay. He picked it up and worked the lever several times. It seemed to be in working order. It was dust-covered, and Steve wouldn't want to fire it right now. That dust could have plugged the barrel. Just as soon as he could, he would give the rifle a good cleaning.

Steve picked up his battered valise from the wreckage of the wagon. He didn't have much in it but these few clothes, which were all he had.

He forced his legs for the first few steps, but with each stride the legs seemed to ease up and move better. If he kept on, he was sure to run into somebody. This was virgin land, and it was useless to hope to find a hotel or restaurant. He winced at the thought of the few dollars in his pocket.. He couldn't afford any high prices. He was hungry, and his belly grumbled.

The bruises would be with him for quite a while, but he plodded on doggedly, ignoring the aches as much as he could. He squinted at the sun, estimating its position. He judged the time to be about midafternoon. He tried to keep his mind closed to the worry that was beginning to grow. Surely, he would find somebody before darkness fell.

An hour later, he ran into the first persons he had seen since the run started. A man and woman worked together, evidently trying to firmly establish their claim to the homestead they had chosen. The raw, pine stakes gleamed yellowly in the afternoon sun. How Steve envied them. They had found the land they wanted and every move from now on would further establish their claim.

A jaded horse had been set free of the buggy's shafts. It was listlessly cropping at the prairie grass. The two people had erected a sad tent. The rents from long wear showing plainly. Even if he had had the opportunity, Steve wouldn't have picked this piece of land. First, he didn't see any evidence of water, and from what he could surmise water lay a good distance away. Without any adequate shelter, this was going to be a piece of hell in the summertime. He shrugged. It was none of his affair. If they were satisfied, who was he to question their judgment?

The man had his back toward Steve, and the man hacked away at some brush. Evidently, the ax was dull, for it took several strokes to fell a small trunk. The woman was hunkered over a spot just before the tent. She had leveled the ground, yanking out tufts of grass. Her grubby hands and broken fingernails showed how hard this work was. Now, she was making a circle of small stones, selecting each from a pile she had gathered. Steve imagined she was preparing a spot for the evening's campfire.

He cleared his throat and said tentatively, "Howdy."

Neither was aware of his presence until he spoke. The woman squealed in alarm, and the man turned, whipping an angry face toward Steve.

He was a stoop-shouldered man, and by the sullen lines in his face, Steve suspected life hadn't dealt easily with him.

He came toward Steve, brandishing his ax. "What the hell are you doing here?" he asked in a blustering tone.

"I only want some information," Steve said mildly. "Do you know where I can find—"

The man cut him short. "Do you think that excuse is going to fool me?" he sneered. "You're only trying to throw us off guard, then jump us. Ma, grab that shotgun. It's leaning right inside the tent. Maybe that scattergun will convince him I mean what I say."

The woman darted into the tent and reappeared almost instantly. The shotgun muzzle was pointed at the ground. Steve drew before she had a chance to swing up the gun.

"You want your woman shot?" he demanded coldly. "Tell her to drop that gun."

The man blanched, and a white line appeared around his lips. "Do as he says, Ma," he said shakily.

The shotgun fell from the woman's soiled fingers.

"What are you going to do now, Mister?" the man asked.

Steve's anger showed in his thinned lips. "Not what you're so fearful of," he snapped. "Though I could kick you off this claim now."

The man stared at him with sick eyes. "You could," he admitted hollowly. "I guess we couldn't stop you."

Good humor returned to Steve. This confrontation was ridiculous. He dropped the gun back into its holster. "I told you the truth. I only stopped here to ask information. I wrecked my wagon and lost my team. Where's the most likely spot I can find people?"

The man gulped and now he was eager to oblige. "I'd say you can find some people about ten miles ahead. Last night, I heard people talking about settling Guthrie. My woman and I don't want a lot of people around."

Steve nodded his thanks. "I don't think you have any

need to worry," he said caustically. "You picked a damned poor piece of land."

The man colored at the criticism. "What's wrong with it?" he demanded.

"First, I'd say you're quite a way from water. Until you dig a well, you'll be lugging water. Second, there's no firewood in sight. Mister, I think you'll be spending most of your time doing the chores you'll have to do just to survive."

He touched a finger to the brim of his hat. "Sorry, ma'am," he apologized. "Didn't mean to frighten you."

He looked back after a dozen strides. The man and woman were yelling at each other.

Steve grinned bleakly. He would say the man was catching hell for his lack of foresight. It would be a long-lasting hell. Every time the woman had to lug water and tote in firewood, her temper would rise again. Steve chuckled.

If this contact was a harbinger of the kind of people he would find in Oklahoma, Steve didn't want any part of them. An old saying of his father's popped into his mind: once bitten, twice shy. He lengthened his stride. If somebody had plans to establish a town, Steve better get there as soon as he could. Ten miles was a long way on an empty belly.

CHAPTER 2

THE farther Steve went, the more people he saw dotted about the prairie, but never in numbers to even suggest a town might be forming. No, these were the early stoppers, the people who had settled on pieces of land to their liking. In every case, they had chosen better pieces of land than the man and woman with whom he had had an altercation. These people had chosen sites on creeks or very near water, and sizable timber was within easy reach.

He plodded doggedly on by them. Once, one of them hailed him, and Steve waved a hand in return. He had no desire for closer contacts; not after the first unhappy encounter.

The sun was dipping lower in the western sky, and fatigue was beginning to build up in his legs. But the increasing hunger was worse. It gnawed at his vitals with savage, rat teeth.

He came to a creek and worked down it, looking for a simple place to cross. Back a way, this creek looked deep. He came to a low-water bridge, and by the tracks it was well known. Steve splashed through the creek, the water coming barely up to his ankles. On the other side, he stomped his feet to dislodge the mud.

He had hardly started again when a voice hailed him. He looked all around, trying to locate it.

"Over here," the voice called.

Through a break in the brush lining the creek, Steve saw a rude camp. Two men were seated at a blazing fire, and another waved imperatively to Steve.

"Come on in," he yelled.

Steve detected no animosity in the voice. He turned cautiously toward the rude camp. There was no harm in finding out what the man wanted.

The three men must have been here for quite a while, for they had erected a rough lean-to of brush. The speaker was a man of impressive proportions. He was a jolly man, for he laughed constantly, and each time his belly shook. The second one was just the opposite: thin as a fence rail. The third one was no more than a lad. Steve guessed him to be around fifteen. Like the thin man, he was sullenfaced. This was an odd company to be traveling together, and Steve wondered curiously about them for a moment.

The thin man stirred something in a pot suspended from a tripod over the flames. The aroma reached Steve's nostrils, and saliva ran in his mouth.

"What's on your mind?" he asked.

"Saw you on foot and just wondered about you," the fat man replied. He threw back his head, and laughter rolled out of his mouth.

Steve resented that laughter. He didn't see anything about his predicament that was so amusing.

The fat man dried his eyes and asked, "Did you have some trouble?"

Maybe there was a note of sympathy in the words, and it softened Steve. "Some," he admitted. "Smashed up my wagon and lost my team. I'm trying to walk my way in."

The fat man shook his head. "Hell of a note. How about a bite to eat?" A pudgy hand rose, stopping possible refusal. "We've got plenty. You're more than welcome."

That sounded genuine enough, and all of Steve's resentment vanished. "Don't mind if I do." He sat down eagerly beside the fire.

The thin man's sullenness didn't vanish, and Steve sensed a deep-seated animosity. Against him or the fat man? Steve pondered over the question.

The thin man ladled out the stew on a tin plate and handed Steve a battered spoon.

Steve dug in, not trying to hide his hunger. That delicious aroma from the pot was false advertisement, for the stew didn't live up to its promise. The chunks of meat were half cooked, and the potatoes were almost raw. The thin man handed Steve a chunk of stale bread. Steve nodded his thanks without stopping. He wasn't complaining about his meal. A man's hunger savored any food.

He didn't object to a second helping. When he finished, he wiped his mouth with the back of his hand, then glanced at the fat man.

"Can't tell you how much I appreciate this, Mr. ——" He paused to let the man fill in his name.

"Call me Kelly," the fat man answered. He snickered as though he was highly amused, and the laugh was just as offensive as before.

The thin man and the boy cast startled looks at Kelly. Their mouths were half open as though they wanted to protest. Kelly's eyes bored into them, and their mouths closed weakly.

Steve stood and brushed off the seat of his pants. "I'd like to do something to repay you," he offered. "I could haul in some wood."

Kelly made a deprecatory motion with his hand. "Won't be necessary."

Steve half turned to leave. "Well, if that's the way you feel about it. I can't tell you how much I'm obliged."

"Hold it," Kelly said sharply.

The harshness of the tone checked Steve, and he whipped his head about. His eyes narrowed, and his jaw muscles bunched at what he saw. Kelly held a derringer in his fat palm. His hand almost encompassed the small gun, but the bore of the muzzle looked bigger than a tunnel. A derringer was a highly inaccurate weapon at any considerable distance, but in the half-dozen feet between them, Kelly couldn't miss.

Kelly snickered again, the sound scraping across Steve's skin like a piece of glass over a blackboard. "You asked what you could do to pay for your meal," Kelly said. "I just thought of something. Empty your pockets after you drop your guns on the ground."

Steve stared at him. This was a bad dream, but it was no ill-flavored joke. Kelly meant every word he said. Steve desperately sought a way to save the few dollars he had. They weren't enough to take a chance with his life, but still the resentment remained. The way this whole matter happened was enough to set his teeth on edge.

He reversed the rifle, presenting the stock as he stepped forward a pace.

"Watch yourself," Kelly warned, his eyes alert.

"I was just going to hand you this," Steve said, offering the butt of the rifle.

"I told you to drop it on the ground," Kelly snapped.

Steve shrugged. "If that's the way you want it." Steve bent forward until his hand was only a few feet above the ground. "Good rifle," he said casually. "I hate to throw it around."

"Just drop it," Kelly said impatiently.

Steve's right hand gripped the barrel of the rifle. He suddenly whipped it forward, sending it spinning end over end.

Kelly's reactions were slow, and he didn't pick up Steve's motion until it was too late. The whipping rifle barrel whacked him across a shin. Kelly yelped in pain. He fired just as Steve left the ground in a long, shallow dive. Steve hit the ground and rolled. He heard the small sound of the slug as it hit the ground behind him, but that sullen roar of the small gun was loud. He pulled his pistol while he rolled and came up on one knee. The sights were centered on that immense belly, and he pulled the trigger.

Kelly's eyes bulged under the shock of the bullet. His mouth sagged open, and he made hoarse, guttural, choking sounds. He rose on his toes, struggling to stay on his feet. The derringer dropped from his hand, and he leaned forward. He lost his balance and his great weight sent him crashing to the ground.

Steve's eyes studied the prone figure. Kelly might not be dead, but there would be no further threat from him.

Steve whipped his head about and covered the thin man and boy with the pistol's muzzle.

"Don't," the thin man squalled, throwing up his hands in desperate entreaty. "We weren't together."

The boy shook in abject terror, his face ashen. His lips shook so that Steve doubted he could even speak.

"We're not armed," the thin man begged. He held his hands wide from his side.

"All right," Steve said, and stood. Anger still shook him in its grip.

"Turn around slow," a crisp voice said. "And drop that gun."

Steve slowly turned. A hard-faced man sat on a dun horse. He held a pistol leveled on Steve, and the sunlight glistened from the badge pinned to his vest. In the midst of his passion, Steve hadn't even heard the rider approach.

CHAPTER 3

"I said drop that gun," the officer snapped.

Steve opened his fingers and let the pistol drop. This mess kept getting worse. This was a law officer; surely, he would listen to reason.

"I didn't hear you," Steve said.

"Too engrossed in shooting a man?" the officer asked. He glanced at Kelly's figure, and a slight frown touched his face.

"Listen," Steve said frantically. "It's not like it looks. I stopped by here, and Kelly invited me to eat with them. When I offered to do something in payment, he pulled a derringer and ordered me to drop my guns and empty my pockets."

He saw disbelief firm the officer's face, and his worry increased. "Goddamn it! Ask them. They saw it all." That was unwise, and he knew it the moment the words were out. These two were with Kelly. What if they backed up Kelly, turning against him?

The officer put penetrating eyes on the man and boy. "You saw it all?"

The man nodded. "We sure did. Me and my boy had just staked out a piece of land. That fat one came up shortly after and said he was taking over. He had a gun to back it up. I saw this one coming across the creek, and the fat one warned me not to say anything. He invited the stranger in and, after feeding him, he tried to rob him." He jerked his head toward Steve. "He moved quicker than a cat. He was carrying a rifle, and he slung it at the fat man, hitting him across the shins. Then he dived from his feet and rolled. The fat man was far too slow. He got off one shot, but it was behind this man. Then this one came up to one knee, and his gun was in his hand. He fired without seeming to aim, and he caught the fat man at the breastbone."

The officer holstered his gun. "His story fits with yours." His tone changed. "Who was he?"

"He called himself Kelly."

The marshal swung down. "Never heard of him. By the way, I'm Marshal Dixon. I was assigned to take over Oklahoma City."

Steve grinned weakly. His face felt wet, and he was shaking inwardly. "Never happier to see anybody in my life."

Dixon's lips twitched. "I can imagine."

He walked over to the fat man and toed him over. "His name isn't Kelly."

"You know him?"

"He's Lester Milligan. I've had a few run-ins with him. He's done time for petty thievery. Looks like he was trying to climb up." He frowned at the thin man. "What's your name? This your boy?"

"I'm Hiram Bollins." Bollins was eager to talk. "After Ma died, the boy and me wanted to get into a new country." He gestured vaguely. "You know, a new start. We made the run and picked out this place." He was a weak man, and it showed in his face and his gestures. "You think I was wrong?"

"Not wrong," Dixon replied. "Just the way you went about it. Didn't you bring any weapons with you?"

"I never fired a gun in my life," Bollins said slowly.

Dixon's nod was a confirmation of what he thought. "I'll give you the best advice I can. You better get a gun and learn to use it as quick as you can. For quite a while, this is going to be a pretty wild country. You'll see a lot of people like Lester Milligan. If you don't protect yourself, they'll strip you."

Bollins squinched his eyes together, and his lips were a thin, bloodless line. He glanced at his son, and his eyes were harried. "I'll take your advice to heart, Marshal."

Dixon glanced at Steve. "What's your reason for being here?"

"I made the run, too," Steve answered. "I smashed up my wagon and it killed my team. I was trying to walk in."

Dixon shook his head. "You're a little late, Mr. ———" he hesitated.

"Steve Truman," Steve filled in the space.

"I won't have to worry about you," Dixon said. "You've already proven you can take care of yourself. My new post is where Oklahoma City is supposed to rise. I can give you a lift, if you're going there."

"I'm obliged," Steve said gravely. "Any direction would be a help." He bent and retrieved his rifle and pistol.

"You pretty handy with those?"

Steve nodded with no effort to boast. "I kept meat on the table."

Dixon climbed onto the dun and removed a boot from the stirrup so that Steve could step into it. "All set?" he asked when Steve was settled.

"All set, Marshal." Steve knew an instantaneous liking for this man. Dixon's presence had lifted him out of what could have been a sticky mess.

"What do you plan on doing?" Dixon asked over his shoulder.

"Anything I can find," Steve replied. "And that better be quick. It don't look like I'm going to get any land."

Dixon chuckled. "Down that low, eh?" He rode several paces in silence. "I could use a deputy," he said almost matter-of-factly. "Pay's pretty poor. But a man can get along on it."

Steve was momentarily speechless. "Are you offering me a job?" he asked hoarsely.

"I know you can use a gun and think your way out of a jam. It takes nerve to face a man with a gun on you. I don't need any better recommendation."

At Steve's silence he said impatiently, "Do you want the job or not?"

"I want it," Steve burst out. My God, he was in luck. Without any foreseeable prospects, he was offered a job that would give him standing. He didn't care what the pay was; at least, he could eat.

"It could be a dangerous job," Dixon warned. "This land rush has filled the territory with the worst scum in the country. Most of them would shoot or stab you, if they thought you had a quarter on you."

Steve nodded gravely, though Dixon didn't see the gesture. Steve already had proof of that. Milligan had tried to rob him without even knowing if it was worthwhile.

"Are you trying to talk me out of this job?" There was laughter in Steve's tone.

Dixon shook his head. "I just want you to know what you're facing."

Steve chuckled. "You still can't talk me out of it."

"It's going to be an unstable land for a while," Dixon went on. "A kind of madness started all this, and until time settles the people down, that madness will go on. It started out with lawlessness. Milligan was an example of that. I don't know how many people tried to beat the opening time limit, sneaking across the line, trying to locate a claim before others could get in." His voice grew gloomy. "The law's going to have quite a struggle against the sooners."

"You mean you're going to try to find and throw them out?" Steve's tone was incredulous.

Dixon nodded. "Something like that. The local law will be new and weak. They won't be able to do much except keep surface order. Oh I'm not saying that everybody is there illegally, but a big percentage of them are. If things get too hot for them in the opened territory, all they have to do is to slip across into Hell's Fringe. That's a thin strip of land between the Indian reservations and the opened-up territory. The local law won't follow them there. That will be turned over to the United States marshals."

Steve chuckled again, and Dixon asked suspiciously, "That amuse you?"

"A little," Steve admitted. "You've got to admit it makes for an interesting life."

"It could also make for a short one," Dixon said grimly. "Just wanted you to know what you'll be up against."

"I'll keep it in mind," Steve said calmly.

CHAPTER 4

Dixon had sworn in Steve after they reached Oklahoma City. It was a short ceremony and certainly not earth-shattering, but Steve felt a tremendous pride as he pinned on the badge.

The memory of that ceremony kept flashing through Steve's mind as he walked along. So far, it had been anything but a dull life. He was one of six deputies Dixon had hired, and Steve had made his share of arrests. Twice, he had had to wound men, and he was glad that he didn't have to kill them.

Steve guessed he was getting along okay, for Dixon had never reprimanded him. But then, Dixon was always a taciturn man. Steve didn't know what it would take to make Dixon talk.

It happened one day, as Steve came around a corner. Dixon was down in the street, both hands grabbing a wound in a leg that spurted blood. It must have happened very recently, though as yet it had drawn no crowd. Several people, however, were beginning to run that way. An ugly brute of a man stood over Dixon, a pistol leveled at his head.

"Got you this time," he gloated. "You bastard, I told you I would one of these days."

Steve was across the street and hurriedly took in the scene. Dixon's gun was still in his holster. Steve heard everything the man said, then the click of a cocked hammer. He didn't try to yell; he had to avoid anything that might disturb the attacker enough to pull the trigger.

"Beg hard enough, and I might let you live a minute longer," the man said.

"Go to hell," Dixon said through clenched teeth.

Steve drew his pistol, hurrying the motion, but not too fast to make the motion ragged. The trouble was that he didn't know how much time he had. Just a touch of the trigger finger, and Dixon's head would be blasted apart.

Steve aimed and pulled the trigger. The report of the gun echoed up and down the street. The second shot came almost immediately. It came from the man, standing over Dixon, but his gun was pointed at the street. Steve saw the gouge of the slug. His bullet hit the big brute in the neck. The impact knocked him forward a stumbling pace. He managed momentarily to hold his balance, and he swung a startled face toward Steve. The hatred in those dying eyes hit Steve like a great, searing wind. But the man could do nothing about his hatred, for the gun had already dropped from his slackening fingers.

He collapsed all at once, falling in a lifeless heap in the street.

Steve hurried to where Dixon lay. People were coming on a dead run, and they were less than a quarter of a block away.

Steve yelled at them, bellowing like a mad bull. "Stay back," he called. He didn't want all these curiosity seekers crowding in around Dixon. Steve still held the gun, and he brandished it fiercely.

He had already established a minor reputation in the use of a gun, and his threat and fierce demeanor stopped and held them as effectively as though he had thrown up a barrier.

"I had to shoot him in the back, Sam," Steve grimaced. "First time I ever did that."

Dixon's face was pale and set from the pain. "I'm damned glad you did," he said through clenched teeth. "I thought my time was up. I'll never be able to repay you."

"Forget it. I'd say we're about even for what you did for me, giving me the job."

"The two things don't balance at all, Steve."

"We'll argue about it later. Who was he?" He glanced at the inert bulk.

"Dobie Edison. A confirmed thief. Steal anything he could get his hands on. My testimony sent him up for five years. They dragged him out of the courtroom, screaming he'd pay me back." Dixon grunted and shifted his position to ease the pain. "He damned near did."

"How bad is it, Sam?"

"Bad enough," Dixon grunted. "Dobie made one bad mistake." A wave of pain washed across his face, and he caught his breath.

Steve waited patiently. Dixon would go on when he was able.

"He came up behind me. I didn't see him. He could have stopped me for good, but he wanted me to know who he was. He shot me in the leg so he could gloat about it."

"That evens up for me shooting him in the back," Steve commented. The watching crowd was pushing forward, and he yelled savagely, "Get back. I won't tell you again."

The man who was doing most of the pushing was half as big as a house. "Who do you think you're talking to?" he demanded.

The man standing beside the big one pulled at his arm and caught his attention. He said something, and the big man blinked. "You're sure that's Steve Truman?"

The speaker nodded. The belligerence faded rapidly, and the big man stepped back. "Get back," he barked. "You heard what Mr. Truman said."

Steve didn't allow his bleak grin to show. So a reputation could be helpful. This was better than having to use force to emphasize his command.

The doctor was a couple of blocks away, but Dixon wasn't a big man. "You," Steve pointed at the huge man. "I need you to help me get the marshal to the doctor's."

"Whatever you say," the big man replied quickly. He stepped forward, and Steve said, "I'll take his feet." He didn't have to ask if the man could handle the rest of Dixon's weight. He was big enough to have easily carried Dixon all by himself.

Steve kept telling the man to slow down. Steve didn't want Dixon jostled any more than was necessary. Even the gentlest handling was costing Dixon. Every time Steve glanced at him, the marshal's mouth was a tight line, and he was too pale. He was sweating profusely when they carried him into the doctor's office.

Doc Neblins was a fussy old man, but he was good at his trade. Steve had seen him work on wounded men before. Neblins should be good with gunshot wounds; he'd had enough practice.

"How bad is it, Doc?" Steve asked anxiously.

"I've seen worse," Neblins grunted after he made his examination. "He's lost a lot of blood. Oh he'll recover, but it'll be a long time before he uses that leg well."

"Take the best care you can, Doc. I'll be back to check on him later in the day."

Steve walked to the door with the big man. "Stop me the next time you see me," Steve said. "I owe you a drink." He stuck out his hand, and it was swallowed by the big paw. "Who do I thank for this help?"

That great moon face split in a broad grin. "Jude Kingsley. I haven't been in town long. I never did appreciate anybody yelling at me."

"Forgotten." Steve grinned in return. He thought his hand would be crushed under the tremendous pressure. "I appreciate what you did, Jude." He jerked his head toward where Neblins still worked over Dixon. "That man means a lot to me."

"You showed it. It's a rough town, ain't it?"

"As rough as I want it," Steve replied. "You've run into it already?" With Kingsley's size, Steve would have thought that quarrelsome men would avoid him.

"I've had a few clashes." Kingsley spit into the dust. "But I don't carry no weapons on me. If a man wants to pick a quarrel with me, he's got to use his hands. So far, I haven't run into many who did."

"They're wise." Steve chuckled. "I've got to be getting back to my rounds." He nodded to the big man and moved on down the street.

That had been three months ago, and Dixon still limped. The leg was tender. Steve tried to keep the burden of the office off of him. Dixon had never thanked him again, but he showed in every possible way how he felt about Steve. The bond between them didn't need words to nourish and strengthen it.

Steve moved slowly down the street. Oklahoma City was only six months old, and for the life of him, Steve couldn't see much improvement. Oh a lot of the tents had been replaced with sturdier buildings. Local law had been established, but it was barely keeping its head above the troubled waters. The federal marshal had his own office in a plank building, and so far the jail constructed of logs had been able to hold every prisoner put into it. It was the character of the people that didn't show much improvement. Everywhere he looked, he saw men with ammunition belts strapped around their waists, and they usually carried one or two .45s in holsters. A lot of them must feel they needed additional security, for they also carried rifles. It was a raw, violent town with too many people ready to break into savage action at the slightest pretext.

Main Street was the principal business section. The residential district was located on the highlands that stretched north. Most of the decent, law-abiding citizens lived there. They tended to their businesses, seeking only to make an honest living. But the town would remain in an unsettled condition until the decent element grew sick of the lawless element and put forth a concentrated effort to run the toughs out of town.

Steve now stood on the dividing lines. The honky-tonk district, the dance halls, the cribs and dives were located on the south side. Almost every night saw another violent quarrel with one of the adversaries either killed or wounded. It kept the local law busy, and they weren't doing a too efficient job. The offender usually slipped out of town before the law's search, running for Hell's Fringe. The local law wouldn't go in after him. It left the choice up to the federal marshal's office, and it kept Dixon's force busy.

Steve walked past the gambling houses centered on the street fronting the railroad and depot. The section ran for four or five blocks. It was known in town as Gamblers' Row. Whatever game of chance a man wanted, he could find it in those sleazy buildings. Street fakers and medicine shows filled every cranny to sop up whatever dribbled down to them.

Steve turned, walked into one of the larger places and pushed through the throng. His eyes rested lazily on the huge green baize-covered tables. The large tables had three-inch rails, similar to a billiard table. Small pyramids of money, gold, silver and paper were piled on the tables. Gambling fever flushed every face around the table. The poor, damn fools, Steve thought indifferently. He had no idea how many people came into this room during a day, but the number must be in the hundreds. If he wanted a sure bet, he could bet that only a few walked out with any money in their pockets, let alone any profit.

A guard was posted at one side of the biggest table with two :45s in front of him. He coolly watched the crowd pushing against the table. His hands were never far away from those guns. Anybody who made a foolish move toward that money would be dead before he could blink his eyes.

The guard recognized Steve and grinned mockingly at him. Steve had been in here dozens of times before, looking for an offender. Not once had he been successful, and nobody offered him any information. Everybody had conspired to spirit the lawbreaker out of one of the numerous doors, leaving Steve fuming. The guard belonged in that category.

Steve returned the grin. He had learned months ago to hold his temper. If he did, he came out on top most every time.

He got several scowls, and hot eyes looked at him. But no one attempted to speak. Most everybody had learned some time ago that Steve's temper could be on a thin leash. Snap that leash, and all hell broke loose.

This place, like dozens like it in town, was crowded day and night. False excitement buoyed the people. Steve could understand that. They had nothing to occupy them until the ownership of their lots was firmly established. Games of chance helped eliminate their boredom.

Looking at the crowd, Steve wondered often if Oklahoma City would ever settle down. If he had to bet right now, he would say no. The booming town had collected such a motley crowd—gamblers, cutthroats, refugees, bootleggers and crooks of lesser status. Almost every state in the Union was represented; the Kansas jawhawker, the Arkansas Reuben glue, known by his shaking from the buck ague, and the Missouri puke. Steve was one of the latter, though he didn't consider himself as one of the kind the historians wrote about. The Missouri puke is so vile his own native state has puked him out. The Texas ranger and the Illinois sucker mingled with all the others. There were representatives of every phase of crime. Steve saw and identified horse thieves, train robbers, hijackers, bank robbers, yeggman and brand blotters. After a few months on this job, they stuck out like sore thumbs. If Steve couldn't identify them from the wanted posters, they had been pointed out to him by Dixon. Oh there were some honest tradesmen in this restless crowd. Steve picked out bronco busters, sheep herders, cow punchers, bull whackers and range riders. They made an honest dollar at their work. But would that honesty last? Steve often wondered about that. If they spent much time in one of these places, their few dollars would be gambled away. Then what did they turn to? That was an interesting question. With all the money in plain sight, it would be hard to resist temptation. Then another or a dozen would join the ever-growing crowd of lawbreakers. It makes my job secure, Steve thought wryly.

Now and then, he nodded to a person he knew. There was no loosening in his face, or a welcoming in his eyes. They respected him, but they displayed no fondness. He saw Piute Charley, Alibi Pete, Comanche Hank, Poker Jim, Rattlesnake Jack and Cactus Sam. Those flamboyant names were indicative of the men who wore them. They were devoid of scruples and fast and accurate with a gun. Steve had seen them toss a half dollar in the air and hit it squarely with a quickly drawn gun, three times out of five. Lord, Steve thought, how did an honest man ever hope to earn a living? With the arrival of every honest man, there were dozens of con artists waiting to pounce on him. Steve had talked often about the enormity of the job an honest lawman had on his hands.

"Quit thinking about it," Dixon had advised him. "Or you'll drive yourself crazy."

Steve hadn't disagreed openly with him, but it all seemed so hopeless.

Steve finished his tour through the gambling house and stepped back on the street. He hadn't seen anyone he wanted. His head was filled with faces of wanted men. Dixon had something Steve would have to acquire: patience. Right now, it looked as though that was one trait he would never develop. It was like trying to dip the ocean dry with a spoon. For every crook arrested, a dozen more crawled out of the woodwork to take his place.

Steve scowled at the setting sun. It was about time to get back to the office to see that those three prisoners were fed. If he or one of the other deputies weren't there to do it, Dixon would feel obliged to take care of them. Getting around was still difficult for him.

Three more of the slimy bastards caught and held for a

while, Steve thought in disgust. Until they were sent away to prison, or gotten a release by some clever lawyer, Steve would have them on his hands. His jaw hardened. There was another way of getting a release. Some crooked judge would sit on their trial and find the evidence insufficient to hold them. Steve shook his head. Maybe he was too young to have such a sour outlook on life, but he had seen just that happen too often to be overly optimistic that the system would ever improve. Thank God, the trial for those three would come up next week. Then maybe he would have Black Mask Charley, his brother Elmer and the hanger-on, Odie Parnell, taken off his hands. He snorted at the thought of them. They had started out as minor criminals and rapidly worked themselves into prominent status. They were caught for their involvement in a claim-jumping scheme. The body of the real owner had been found in a shallow grave. Black Mask Charley had once stood too close to a blast from a pistol, and the powder specks had penetrated his cheek to leave a permanent mark. Elmer didn't have a brain in his head. He adored his brother Charley Divens. Odie Parnell had hung around them since he was a kid. He didn't have any more ability to think than Elmer did. Steve shook his head. Too bad that the shot that disfigured Charley's face hadn't been better aimed.

Steve shrugged, trying to get rid of the unhappy impressions. Oh well, it would be over after the trial was held. No matter how clever a lawyer was, or how blind the judge, they wouldn't be able to topple obvious evidence.

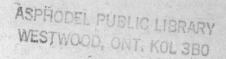

CHAPTER 5

OLD JAKE the jailer turned his head at the sound coming from the cells. Those Divens and that Odie Parnell were raising hell again. "Shut up," he yelled furiously. With each passing day, those three were causing more of a ruckus.

He opened a desk drawer with a trembling hand and pulled out a bottle. It had been three days since he'd had a drink, and it showed in his drawn face and haunted eyes.

He took a long pull from the bottle and shuddered as the potent stuff went down. God, that whiskey was so raw that he would be surprised if it didn't eat his stomach away. He waited until the fiery burn eased, then took another cautious swallow. Again, he shut his eyes and shuddered. He opened his mouth and gasped against the fiery wash. Ah, that was better. He looked at his hands; they were fairly steady. Marshal Dixon didn't like his drinking on the job, and Jake had desperately tried to quit. But when his nerves became too frayed, this was the only thing he knew that would quiet them.

This was a rotten job and the pay poor, but what else could an old man find to do? The only solution to his problem was not to let Dixon catch him drinking.

He started as the yelling began again. "Goddamn it," he screamed. "I told you to shut up."

The yelling didn't stop, and Jake strapped on his gun belt. "I'll shut you up," he muttered. He knew that was vain boasting, though he would like nothing better than to plug those three. But regardless of their record, Dixon wouldn't stand for that.

Jake walked down the cage-lined corridor until he reached the last cell. All three of them stood gripping the bars and yelling.

"Shut up," Jake raged. "I'm not coming back here again to tell you."

Charley Divens was a fearsome-looking man with the blue-gray pigmentation in his left cheek. He was an ugly man, his eyes set too close together under heavy brows. Some blow to the jaw had broken it, and the bone hadn't healed properly. It gave his face a queer, twisted appearance.

"If we don't," Dixon snarled, "what will you do?" He delighted in taunting this old man.

"By God, I could put a hole in you," Jake howled, goaded beyond his limit.

"You wouldn't dare," Divens taunted. "Marshal Dixon would come down on you harder than a hen after a bug."

His grin showed broken teeth. "Or haven't you heard? The marshal's against murder no matter who does it."

Elmer and Parnell howled their delight. "That's telling him, Charley."

Jake thought he would choke with rage. "Next week, I'll be rid of you three. I hope I get to see you hang."

Divens' eyes changed color as he glared murderously at Jake. "You'll never see that," he snapped. "You better find out what's holding up our supper. We're not animals Dixon can lock up and go away and forget."

"It's barely suppertime," Jake said with deep disgust. "Don't be doing any more yelling, or I'll tell the marshal what you said."

"You go ahead and do that," Divens called after him.

Jake was still fuming when Steve came in a few minutes later, carrying a tray loaded with food.

"They been bitching their heads off," Jake raged. "About their meal being late."

"They must be getting scared as their trial gets closer and closer," Steve observed. "All of us will be glad to see them gone. Come with me and cover me when I take the food inside the cell."

He looked curiously at him. "You been drinking, Jake? You sure sound like it."

Jake shook his head. He didn't want Steve to know. He didn't know how blabber-tongued Steve was. "I ain't been drinking," he said sullenly.

Steve set the tray on top of the desk. He unbuckled his belt and handed it and his gun to Jake. Steve sniffed suspiciously. "It sure smells like you've been drinking, Jake. Keep at it, and you'll wind up losing your job."

"Mind your own business," Jake snarled. The realization of his defiance scared him. Steve had been a good friend. Jake didn't want to alienate him. "I didn't mean that, Steve. Sometimes, this job gets on my nerves."

"I know," Steve said soothingly. He could appreciate the bind Jake was in. Old age had him in its relentless grip, and there was nothing to look forward to. His pay was so small that it was a wonder he ever got enough money to buy a bottle. "You just be careful, Jake," he advised.

Jake felt a lump rise and lodge in his throat. "I will," he said earnestly. "You've been a good friend, Steve."

Steve picked up the tray. "Forget it."

He walked down the corridor ahead of Jake. "Keep an eye on them," he ordered.

Jake bobbed his head. "I will," he promised.

The three in the cell saw Steve and set up a clamor. "What slop have you brought us today?" Charley Divens asked derisively.

"Keep your mouth shut," Steve advised, "or I'll dump this on the floor."

Divens' face turned sullen with rage. "We ain't no animals," he protested. "You got no call to treat us any way you please."

"Then quit acting like animals," Steve said calmly. He unlocked the door, glanced at Jake to be sure he was alert, swung open the door, then stepped inside. He saw something flash in the prisoners' eyes. "Go head," he said easily. "Try something. Jake's watching you. He's got orders to shoot you at the first wrong move. I'd enjoy seeing it."

Their heads turned toward Jake. He held a cocked pistol.

"If you think he can't hit you at this distance, go ahead and try it," Steve jeered. This wasn't the first time for this byplay. Three or four times a week, Steve had seen that calculating look in their eyes. These were desperate men. The closer they came to their trial, the more frantic they became.

Steve nodded approvingly at the change of expression coming into their faces. "Better," he approved. "You know it doesn't make a damned bit of difference whether we shoot or hang you."

He chuckled at the murderous futility that washed over their faces. "At least you can still think."

Charley Divens cursed him until he was breathless. "Just because you bastards wear badges, you think you can kick us around as you please. You just wait. We'll get even with every one of you. That includes Dixon." He jerked a thumb at the watchful jailer. "Yes, and that old coot."

Steve placed the tray on a bunk. "Why don't you just eat and shut up?"

Divens moved to the tray, looked at it, and disgust touched his face. "Hell, this even smells bad."

Steve's anger showed in a quick flush in his face. "It's the same food all of us eat." He couldn't blame old Jake for growing testy under this constant barrage of abuse.

"Eat it, or throw it on the floor. I don't give a damn," Steve snapped. God, would he ever be happy to be rid of these three.

"I know what you're trying to do," Charley cried. "You're trying to poison us."

Steve had taken all he could stand. "I hope it does," he shouted. He walked back to the door, and Jake advanced to let him out.

"See what I mean?" Jake asked in triumph. "That goes on all the time."

"Hang on, Jake. In less than a week, they'll be gone for good."

"Maybe," Jake said gloomily. "Unless some stupid jury or judge turns them loose."

Steve chuckled. "You're really worked up over them."

Jake shivered. "I'll just be glad when they're gone. Damn, I'd hate to have to run up against them again."

Steve considered that. "I would, too," he said gravely. "If I was unarmed. Those are three bad ones."

He paused at the door. "Don't take any unnecessary chances with them, Jake." He wanted to add some advice about Jake laying off the bottle, then shrugged the impulse aside. Jake had lived long enough to know how to take care of himself.

Steve walked into the marshal's office, and Dixon looked up. "Get them fed?"

"Done," Steve said cheerfully. "It's like feeding savage animals. I always feel better when I get out of there."

Dixon didn't smile at Steve's remark. "I know. It's funny," he mused. "All babies are alike when they're born. Most of them turn out good. But a small percentage of them turn out thoroughly bad. Those three came out of that small percentage."

"Does handling that kind ever bother you?" Steve asked curiously.

"Sure it does. I try to keep from thinking about it as much as I can. Every now and then, it gets to me."

Steve knew what he meant. He hadn't handled that kind nearly as long as Dixon had. What would he be like when he reached Dixon's age? My God, he thought in revulsion. He didn't want to be in this business that long.

"Charley shot off his mouth while I was in there. He said he'd make everybody pay."

"He means it too," Dixon said quietly. "The thing to do is never let him find his chance."

Steve thought of that old jailer and his craving for whiskey. Should he say anything about it to Dixon? No, he decided. Dixon had enough on his mind without adding to the burden he carried.

CHAPTER 6

CHARLEY DIVENS grinned at his cellmates. "You two can stop your worrying."

"I don't see how," Parnell said sullenly. "We're still locked up. All that raving about the food being poisoned has plumb taken away my appetite."

He made an agitated turn about the cell. "I don't think it's so damned smart to rile up everybody. I don't think you were so damned smart from the start. Jumping that old man's claim didn't do us a bit of good."

Elmer turned furiously on Parnell. "Get your mouth off my brother. If things had gone right, you'd profit too. We just got a bad break."

"Leave him be," Divens said complacently. "He'll be kissing my ass when I get us out."

"Talk. Just some more damned talk," Parnell fumed. "I'm sick of—"

"Shut up," Elmer yelled at him. "It won't hurt you none to listen to him."

"I'll have us out of here before midnight," Charley bragged. "Just wait and see. All we've got to contend with is that old man. He's a boozer. I've smelled it on his breath." He lowered his voice. "The idea hit me while I was raving at Truman. I wouldn't try it on him. He's too smart. But that old coot—" He didn't finish that sentence. "Now you just listen and pay attention."

Old Jake emptied the bottle and tried to squeeze the last few drops out of it. He smothered his irritation. Maybe he'd had enough, anyway. He downed the last drop and wiped the back of his hand across his lips.

He glanced uneasily toward the cells. It had been almost two hours since he had heard a sound, and that wasn't natural. Maybe he'd better go back there and see if something was wrong.

He stubbornly shook his head. He needed his head examined. Here he was handed all this peace, and he was complaining.

The yell came so suddenly that he almost jumped out of his chair.

"Jake, Jake," the voice yelled. "Get back here. Something bad's happened."

Jake snorted. Did they think they could pull that on him again? He had been the butt of several of their coarse jokes before.

"Jake," Elmer screamed. "Get back here. I think Charley's dying."

Jake jerked as the words hammered at him. He didn't really believe it, but maybe he'd better go back and see.

He strapped on his gun and took the ring of keys from the nail on a post. He wasn't going to use either. All he was going to do was to take a look, but he would have both items with him if he needed them.

He cautiously approached the cell. Elmer and Parnell were bent over Charley. Charley lay on the floor, writhing and jerking. Jake caught just a glimpse of his mouth. He was foaming like a mad dog.

"What's wrong with him?" Jake asked uneasily.

Elmer turned burning eyes on him. "How in the hell do we know? It hit him shortly after we ate. He grabbed his belly and fell on the floor. Then he started foaming at the mouth. Charley knew what was likely to happen when he accused Truman of poisoning him."

Jake was too rattled to think of asking if the other two had eaten the same food. Oh God, Dixon would be furious if something happened to Charley. Jake's head throbbed unmercifully. He wished he hadn't finished the bottle. His thoughts were all muddled up. He wished he was off this miserable job.

"Don't just stand there," Elmer screamed at him. "See if you can do something for Charley."

Jake shook his head. "I'm no doctor. What could I do?"

"You could try," Elmer said heatedly. His face twisted in anguish. "You can't just stand there and watch my brother die."

The tortured plea got through to Jake. He was beyond lucid thinking. He unlocked the cell door and stepped inside, his gun in his hand.

"I'll keep an eye on you," he threatened. "One false move, and I'll blast you both."

He kneeled beside Charley, his head reeling. By God, he was asked to do too much. How could he help a sick man and still watch the other two?

He bent his head lower. "Charley," he pleaded, "can you tell me what it is?"

Charley mumbled something, but Jake couldn't make out the words. Jake bent his head lower. "Say it slower, Charley," he begged. "I don't understand—"

His eyes widened, and he tried to bring his gun into play. Charley's hands were rising and fastening around his neck. Elmer stepped forward and kicked the gun out of Jake's hand.

The thumbs of Charley's hands dug in deeper. "You crazy old fool," Charley said. "I thought that soap foam would fool you."

The pressure of the thumbs increased. Jake gasped for breath, and his fingers clawed at the hands that were shutting off his breath. His nails tore away skin, trying to release that inexorable pressure, but Charley was too strong. Charley turned him over, and his weight effectively smothered Jake's struggles.

Jake was a weak old man, and the lack of air was turning his face black. A clear thought filtered through his mind: This is a hell of a way to end it all.

Charley held him down, the thumbs never easing that pressure. He held Jake until the last struggle ebbed away, then he grinned up at the two.

"I guess that does it," he said and tentatively released his thumbs, watching for any sign of a return of further resistance. "I told you it'd work," he chortled.

"You sure did," Elmer said, affectionately clasping his brother's shoulder. He looked at Parnell. Parnell's face was dubious. "What's the matter with you?" Elmer snarled.

"We still ain't out of here," Parnell said. A faint shudder ran through him as he looked at the limp body. Death made the old man look very frail. "I was just thinking: When they come in and see him, it'll leave no doubt how the trial will go."

Charley pushed to his feet. "Sometimes I don't know why I put up with you. Pick up that gun, Elmer, and hand it to me."

At the startled flash in Parnell's eyes he said, "We might need it. I sure as hell ain't giving up now."

Parnell licked lips that had suddenly gone dry. "You'd shoot anybody who'd try to stop us?"

Charley bared his teeth. "Bet on it. They can only hang us once." Disgust filled his eyes as he looked at Parnell. "You can stay here and wait for them to come."

Parnell weakly shook his head. "I'm going."

Charley peered cautiously out of the front door. The street was dark, and as far as he could see, it was empty. There had been no noise to draw anybody.

He glanced across the street at the marshal's office, where a dim light burned. Charley grinned wickedly at Parnell. "Want to go over and announce we're loose?"

"Let's get out of here," Parnell moaned.

Charley chuckled fiendishly. "You like being out, don't you, Odie? If you want it to stay that way, just do everything I tell you."

Parnell bobbed his head. Charley was satisfied. Parnell was too scared to think of anything else. Charley never had to worry about Elmer. Elmer went along with anything his brother told him.

"We need horses," Charley said after a moment's reflection. "We'll split up and meet at Asa Babcock's livery stable. It's at the edge of town and doesn't do the business of other places. Look it over close before you go in. We'll join you there."

Those mean little eyes dared Parnell to comment. His teeth shone when it didn't come. "You be damned careful on the way there. If you're picked up, it's your own hard luck."

Parnell was filled with resentment. Charley was always on him, and he rarely picked on Elmer. Did that same warning apply to Elmer? Parnell didn't dare ask.

Asa Babcock came awake in the tackroom and sat bolt upright. His eyesight wasn't what it had once been, but his hearing was still sharp. Was that a horse whinnying in the stable, or was it old age that was beginning to fray his nerves? He sat motionless for a moment. He didn't hear the whinny again. Should he go out and investigate, or just forget he had heard it?

He heard the sound again, a shrill, frightened whinny from one of the horses stabled with him. Oh goddamn it, he thought testily. Something was after his horses. The town was filled with abandoned dogs, and they roamed about, looking for anything they could get to eat. Asa had seen them pack up, and no livestock was safe from one of their hungry, ferocious attacks. He had better check it out. If there was an attack, they could slash and mark a horse before they could be driven away. The owner of the abused horse wouldn't be happy if that happened. Asa couldn't afford to pay for any possible damage.

He pulled on his pants, tugged on his worn boots, and sighed as he stood. Every joint ached. Maybe it would be smart to sell this place. He hadn't been doing the business he expected.

He paused to pick up the ancient shotgun leaning in a corner. He checked the single barrel, knowing he always kept it loaded. A man never lost anything by being careful.

He stepped outside into the shadowy aisle and shuffled down it, pausing at every stall. He didn't see any reason for alarm.

He froze as he heard a slight sound from the far stall. It wasn't a whinny, more like some sort of a scraping sound. The horse snorted in protest at something. Those damned dogs were after an animal.

"Hiyah," he yelled fiercely. "Get the hell out of here." He moved on slowly, his eyes peering to make out something definite in this shadowy aisle. If those were dogs, he'd blast the hell out of them.

He reached the stall and peered over the door. Imagination was all that was bothering him. He didn't see a thing. He started to turn away when the horse bobbed its head and snorted nervously. In the poor light, Babcock saw something that alerted him. The horse's bridle was on, and he was positive he had removed it. The horse's owner said he wouldn't be back until the following day.

Babcock started to enter the stall, and a shadowy form glided up behind him. Something hard poked into his back, and a gravelly voice asked, "Going someplace, old man? Drop that gun."

This had happened to Babcock before, and he was familiar with the feel of a gun in his back. He sighed gustily and lowered the gun.

Another indistinct form slipped up to his left and jerked the shotgun from his hand. Babcock spluttered at the indignity of the rough handling.

"I was going to drop the gun," he said furiously. "This won't do you any good. You won't get anyplace."

"I know you were going to drop it," a cold voice said. The pressure of the muzzle was removed from Babcock's back. He started to turn, and something crashed down on his unprotected head with brutal force.

Just a sigh of a groan slipped from his lips. His legs collapsed as though they were made of string, and he fell limply to the floor.

Parnell didn't like the way the old man fell and said so: "Charley, I think you hit him too hard."

"Good," Charley snarled. He bent over the limp form, listened a moment, then repeated, "Good. We don't have to worry about him coming to and yelling."

Parnell felt a great hollow spreading through him. "You mean he's dead?" he gasped.

Charley didn't like the shakiness in his voice. "Deader than a doornail," he retorted. "Get that sick look off your face." He hit Parnell's shoulder with the heel of his palm, spinning him about. "Pick out a couple more horses. This one will do for me. Elmer, pick up that shotgun," he added as an afterthought. "We might need all the weapons we can get."

They conferred briefly before leaving the stable. "We ride out all at once," Charley decided. "If somebody just happens along and tries to stop us, we'll ride 'em down." He scowled at each in turn, and they nodded. They had no intentions of arguing with him.

"One other thing," he went on. "Remember that little grocery store at the edge of town? From its look, it doesn't get much business. We stop there."

"What for?" Parnell squalled. "To pass the time of day?"

"To pick up supplies, you dummy," Charley said disgustedly. "What do you think we're going to live on?"

"I thought we'd head straight for Hell's Fringe," Parnell said feebly. "The quicker we get there, the safer we'll be."

"We stop at the grocery store," Charley said positively and led the way to the stable's entrance. He reined in his horse and looked up and down the street. "It's clear. Let's go."

Three wildly running horses tore down the street, kicking up pebbles and dust. A yell of exultation kept swelling up in Charley's throat. He'd told all those stupid law bastards that no cell was going to hold him.

Old Pardee Quincy moved aimlessly about the littered little store. His face was heavy with worry. Every cent he had was in this store, and it was failing. He looked about helplessly, trying to see the answer to his problem. He kept the store clean, and he tried to display his merchandise attractively. He kept his prices low, making sure he undersold other stores in town. Still, a few customers came. He couldn't afford to keep this store open much longer. Every day he was open, he was losing money. His suppliers were threatening to cut him off.

What was the answer? It could be because he had picked his location poorly. But he had been a late arrival here, and he grabbed one of the only pieces of property that was available. The rest of the town seemed to be thriving. Maybe it would be wise to sell out and move to another location. That thought brought on another rush of despair. Who would want to buy a failing business?

He turned toward his sleeping quarters in the rear of the store. He might as well turn in. The hour was getting late. Nobody was coming in tonight.

He was facing the door to his quarters when he heard the scrape of boots on the floor. His face brightened. That must be a customer. If a man held steadfast to what he believed, things would change.

He turned, and anxiety tightened his features. He had never seen any of the three men entering the store. They were a seedy-looking lot.

"Yes?" he asked, trying to keep a shakiness out of his voice.

"We need some supplies," one of them said.

A soft little sigh escaped Quincy, and his legs felt weak. Maybe they weren't here to rob him. "What can I do for you gentlemen?" The smile on his face was false and trembling at the edges.

"We're taking a trip," the apparent leader said. "We need supplies. Can you put them in a couple of gunny bags?"

"Why certainly," Quincy replied. "Anything for your convenience. What do you want?"

"We'll stick to canned goods," the leader said. He named can after can, keeping Qunicy hopping about the store to gather them off the shelves.

The pile on the counter grew. Quincy felt happier than he had for a long time.

The leader paused in indecision. "I guess that does it. No, better add a jug of larrup."

Quincy chuckled as he added a jug of molasses to the order. Very few men didn't have a sweet tooth.

He put the cans into the gunny bags, almost filling both of them. He jotted down each item, then bent over his addition. He straightened and said, "That comes to—"

His eyes widened, and his words broke off. The man opposite the counter said softly, "Haven't you recognized me yet?"

Quincy's eyes filled with horror, and his tongue seemed too stiff to move. For the past several minutes, something had been digging at his mind. Should he know the man with the disfiguring patch on his cheek? It came to him suddenly: This was the man whom the whole town was talking about. This was the man who faced a trial for murder.

"I don't know you," he stammered. "I never saw you before." His trembling voice belied the words. He had heard about that black splotch on the man's left cheek. This was Black Mask Charley. This couldn't be. Charley was supposed to be in jail, waiting trial.

"Take the order," Quincy said desperately. "There's no charge."

Charley's grating chuckle filled Quincy's ears. "I don't know you," he repeated frantically. "Take the sacks and get out of here."

That mirthless chuckle filled Quincy's ears again. "So you do know me." His hand lifted from below the counter, and a gun pointed at Quincy. "You know too much for your own good."

"I told you to take the order and leave." Each word came out with great difficulty. "I won't say anything—"

"I know damned well you won't." A finger tightened on a trigger, and flame blasted from the gun's muzzle. At this short range there was no possibility of missing. Quincy's eyes bulged from his head, and he leaned forward. He tried to grab the edge of the counter to retain his balance.

All the strength went out of his hands, and the fingers slipped along the counter. A despairing wail filled his head, but no sound came out. This wasn't the way it should end. The encroaching blackness overcame him, and he fell heavily.

"Jesus Christ," Parnell said, his eyes wide. He leaned far over the counter, stared at the form on the floor, and his voice was shaky. "He ain't moving," he said huskily.

"I didn't intend for him to," Charley said easily.

"For Christ's sake," Parnell burst out. "Why was it necessary to shoot him?"

"To keep him from telling anybody he'd seen us." Charley cocked his head to one side in a listening attitude. The gun's report was loud. It could have been heard for a considerable distance outside.

"You keep running up our bill," Parnell said plaintively.

Charley's lips pulled back in a snarl. "I've told you before: Once you put the first item on that bill, it don't make any difference how many more you add. Grab those sacks and let's get out of here."

Elmer and Parnell each picked up a sack and followed Charley to the door. He stood there and held them back with an outflung arm. He stood there for what seemed an interminable time.

"Don't seem to be anybody around," Charley muttered. "If that shot raised any attention, somebody would be on the way here now. Get mounted up."

He darted into the street, untied his horse, and swung up.

"Are we heading for Hell's Fringe now?" Parnell begged.

"One more stop," Charley said. "Then we ride for the Fringe." He grinned wickedly at the wail that came from Parnell.

CHAPTER 7

STEVE completed his second round of the town and walked into the office. He had some paperwork to catch up on, but he couldn't settle down to it.

He pushed the papers aside and jumped to his feet. He paced restlessly until he caught Dixon's attention.

Dixon lifted his head and asked impatiently, "What's eating on you?"

"I don't know," Steve confessed. "It's just a clammy feeling like something with cold feet is walking across me."

There was no censure in Dixon's glance. As a lawman, he knew the feeling well. Most of the time, the feeling had no basis, but every now and then a lawman wished he had followed his hunch.

"Think you can put it into words?" Dixon asked.

"I keep thinking of bringing supper to the prisoners."

"Have any trouble with them?"

Steve shook his head. "Just a lot of verbal abuse. Charley yelled a lot of threats at me."

"Did you expect him to change?" Dixon asked drily.

"Not really, Sam. I'll be damned glad when he's sent away to prison."

"It could be hanging," Dixon said softly.

"I'd settle for that. He made a lot of wild talk about what he was going to do to get even. I've got a strong hunch it was directed at you."

Dixon shrugged. "Probably; 90 per cent of the criminals yell threats at the man who was responsible for their arrest. You learn to live with it."

"He's still dangerous," Steve insisted.

Dixon nodded without changing expression. "Something else bothering you, Steve?"

Steve kept picking at the thoughts in his mind. Should he say anything about Jake? Steve felt sort of disloyal even thinking of telling Dixon that Jake was boozing. Jake was an old man, and he needed his job.

Dixon squinted keenly at him. "What's eating on you?"

"Do you think Jake is capable of handling his job?" There, it was out, and Steve felt limp inside. He added lamely, "He's pretty old to be handling such dangerous men."

"Ah," Dixon murmured, "so you've noticed it too."

"What are you talking about?" Steve asked crossly.

"His drinking."

Steve's mouth sagged open. Dixon didn't miss much. "And you haven't said anything about it?" he asked feebly.

"I've thought about it several times," Dixon said flatly. "Jake and I grew up together. We've been close." He paused, his eyes far away and unseeing. "It's funny how the bonds between kids last. Jake saved my life once. I never was much of a swimmer. I got in over my head and panicked. Jake pulled me out. He always promised to keep his drinking and his job separate. I didn't want him to lose his job." He spread his hands helplessly. "Was he drinking tonight?"

This hurt Dixon, and Steve didn't see how he could make it much easier. "He was," he said briefly. "I don't know how much, but I smelled it."

Dixon sighed. "I guess I always knew it would come down to this. Let's go over and talk to him about it." He stood and limped over to his hat.

Steve walked across the street with him, keeping his pace slow to match Dixon's limping walk. Dixon didn't say a word on the way over to the jail. His craggy face was pained, and Steve could guess at the troubled thoughts behind it.

They stepped into the jail, and Dixon called, "Jake." The answering silence seemed to be mocking them.

"Where do you suppose he could be, Steve?"

Steve shook his head. "Maybe he stepped out for something. Maybe he ran out of tobacco."

"At this hour?" Dixon scoffed. "If I expected to find him doing anything, it would be sleeping." He raised his voice. "Jake. Where are you?"

There might have been a flash of fear in the eyes that

looked at Steve. The same thought was in Steve's head. Were the prisoners still locked up?

They walked between the cells, and terror gripped Steve as he saw the cell door standing open ahead. He knew the prisoners would be gone before he reached the cell, but he didn't expect to see the figure lying on the floor.

He tried to block Dixon's view, but he wasn't quick enough. "Ahhh," Dixon said. It was a long, drawn-out protest, saying more than any words.

Jake lay on his back, his eyes bulging sightlessly. There was a faint, dark color in the agonized face, and the throat showed evidence of rough handling.

Steve kept still, letting Dixon make the first remark.

"Oh Jake." There was accusation and pain in Dixon's words. He kneeled down beside Jake, his face contorted.

Steve didn't speak while Dixon made his brief examination.

A moment of silent communication passed between Dixon and the dead man. Dixon looked up at Steve, and that harsh composure was back in place on his face.

"They're gone," Steve said to break up the strained moment.

"I knew that when I saw the cell door open," Dixon said frozenly. "Jake was strangled." Again, that flash of hurt showed in his eyes. "It wouldn't have taken much of a struggle. Jake was getting feeble." He grunted as he put his feet under him. His eyes roamed about the cell.

"What are you looking for, Sam?"

"Something that might have drawn Jake in here. He wouldn't have come in here unarmed. But what could it have been?"

That would probably never be answered, Steve thought. But the same question pounded at him. What could it have been?

Dixon limped hurriedly out of the cell. Steve caught up with him before he reached the outer office. "You're not going to leave Jake back there?"

Dixon made an impatient gesture. "I'll send Andrews after his body." Dixon was going through the drawers of the battered old desk. Most of them contained useless junk, the trivia that a man gathered and kept for no real reason.

"Oh," Dixon said tonelessly as he opened the bottom drawer. He pulled out the empty holster and laid it on the desk. "At least we can believe that Jake didn't go in there unarmed."

That answered a partial question. It also posed a tougher problem. Steve could bet that Charley now had the pistol.

"That makes it bad," Dixon said.

Steve was pawing through the papers in the wastebasket. "What's that?" he asked absently.

"Charley being armed," Dixon answered impatiently. "What the hell are you looking for?"

Steve pulled the empty bottle out of the basket. "This." He held it up. "I guess this answers why Jake went into the cell. He wasn't thinking too clear."

A cloud passed across Dixon's eyes. "I could have saved his life by letting him go. Instead, I kept dawdling because I knew he needed the job. Oh goddamn it." He smashed his fist down against the desk.

Steve tossed the bottle back into the basket. "Quit blaming yourself. A man can't go around carrying the mistakes another man makes."

Dixon wearily shook his head. "I know that, Steve. It's time to do a little clear thinking."

He was silent, his eyes narrowed.

"What are you thinking, Sam?"

"The Divens brothers and Parnell are on the loose. We know they've got Jake's pistol. Three wild animals," he muttered. "Did they slip out of town, or are they still holed up here?"

"They won't be as easy to take this time, Sam."

Dixon turned a savage face toward him. "Don't you think I know that?" He sat there, his fingers drumming on the desk. "Where do we start looking?"

"We'd better get at it," Steve remarked.

Dixon nodded and got to his feet. "I'll have to stop by the undertakers and tell him about Jake." At the annoyance in Steve's face he said, "It won't take that much time."

Dixon seemed to be limping more as he moved down the street.

Andrews was a small, scrawny man with a properly concerned face. "Terrible," he kept repeating as Dixon told him about Jake's death. A slash of Dixon's hand cut off another repeat. "Pick him up right away, Andrews. Do what is necessary."

Andrews' mouth was tight and pinched. "Where do you think they are, Marshal?" Frightened eyes looked toward the front door. "Why, they could bust in here at any time."

Dixon grinned mirthlessly. "They could," he agreed. "We don't think they've got horses. Unless somebody was in this with them and furnished horses."

"Terrible," Andrews said again. "We won't know a safe moment until they're captured again."

"That's right," Dixon agreed, that frozen smile in place. "But you can be sure of one thing: The next time they're captured it will be for keeps."

"How's that, Marshal?"

"This murder cinches the case against them," Dixon replied. "No judge or jury will ever free them again. This time, they'll hang."

He grinned frozenly at Andrews and walked toward the door. Dixon heard Andrews' little moan, but he didn't stop, nor turn his head.

"What do we do now?" Steve asked when they got outside.

Before Dixon could answer, a voice hailed him. "Marshal, wait up. We've been looking all over for you."

Dixon and Steve waited until three men pounded toward them. The leading one was a lanky man, panting to recover his breath. "You're damned hard to find," he complained. "We stopped in your office, then looked in the jail." He looked wide-eyed at Dixon. "Do you know you've got a dead man in one of those cells?"

Dixon nodded. "We were just making arrangements for him. What's on your mind?"

"You've got another dead man at the stables."

"Who?" Dixon snapped.

"Asa Babcock. Each of us left a horse with him. We were going to stay in town for a couple of days, but we went broke. Didn't see any sense staying around any longer. Now we can't go back to the ranch. Our horses are gone."

Steve heard Dixon's sharp expletive. "You're sure Asa's dead?"

"He ought to be," the cowboy returned. "His head's crushed."

"Steve, there's your answer as to where the Divens and

Parnell are. They stole those horses. They're no longer in town."

"I thought those three were in jail," the cowboy said.

"They were," Dixon said crisply. "Until this evening. Let's get to that stable."

Quite a few people had gathered at the stable's entrance. Voices clamored at Dixon. "Is it true, Marshal, that old Asa is dead in there?"

"It is," Dixon growled. "Hasn't anybody been in there?"

Apprehensive eyes rolled in taut faces. Dixon picked one of them. "Lykins, you speak up."

"We didn't think we'd better go in, Marshal. If Asa is dead, we didn't want to trample over all the evidence."

Not all the truth, Steve thought scornfully. Most people avoided death whenever possible. They might stand on the fringes but would go no farther unless they were driven.

"Just stay out here," Dixon snapped. "Steve, come with me."

That was an effective barrier erected against the crowd. Even the three cowboys who had lost their horses didn't come in.

Dixon stared bleakly at the crumpled form of Asa Babcock. "Can you read anything into this, Steve?"

"I'd say he was hit on the head. You can see where his skull was crushed. Probably didn't have a chance. They sneaked in and were waiting for him when he came out of the tackroom."

"What do you think did it, Steve?"

"Something heavy. The butt of a gun could do it." Steve's face twisted with a rush of rage. "Probably Jake's gun. Goddamn those bastards. They jump on the helpless, don't they?"

Dixon nodded, his face sober. "It'll be a pleasure to bring them back. Think they took anything else beside the horses?"

Steve pondered over the question. "After horses, they would want weapons next. Didn't Asa have a shotgun in the tackroom?"

Dixon nodded. "I've seen one there several times."

A search of the tackroom turned up no shotgun. "You can bet they got it, Steve." Dixon's face was bleak. "A shotgun and a pistol. They're doing pretty well for being empty-handed when they started."

The small crowd was still outside the stable when Dixon and Steve came out.

"He's dead, isn't he?" somebody called.

"Asa will never be any deader," Dixon said grimly.

"Who did it, Sam?"

"How in the hell would I know?" Dixon growled. "I can't read minds."

The questioner was persistent, and his tone was hostile. "You're not just going to let it drop here?"

Dixon glared at the man. "You let me run my office, will you?"

He limped past the crowd. Steve started to follow him, and the persistent questioner detained him. "Kinda touchy, ain't he?"

"Every right to be," Steve said levelly. "He hasn't got the easiest job in the world, and some damn fool asking questions doesn't make it easier." His cold eyes challenged the man to take offense.

The man flushed and stepped back. Steve lengthened his stride and caught up with Dixon.

"He giving you more jaw?" Dixon asked.

"Yes," Steve said abruptly. "I shut him up."

"I'm glad my job's not elective," Dixon mused. He grinned at Steve's rising eyebrows. "I wouldn't have dared talk that way to a prospective voter."

Steve nodded sober agreement. "Where to now, Sam?"

"Got to stop and tell Andrews he's got more business. Those boys sure went on a spree, didn't they?"

"They're damned dangerous," Steve commented.

"Didn't you know that when we brought them in?"

"Not as much as I do now," Steve retorted.

Andrews' face tightened at the sight of them. "Not more trouble," he said in a plaintive voice.

"Asa Babcock," Dixon said shortly. "You'll find him in his stable."

Andrews was appalled. "You think it was the same men?"

"Could be. Pick up Asa, will you?"

A man burst in through the door, his face agitated. "Marshal, I stopped by your office to tell you something." An accusatory note was in his voice. "You weren't there."

Dixon sighed. More trouble. "What is it, Cooney?"

"You know Quincy's store?" At Dixon's nod, Bill Cooney went on, "It's not the fanciest store in the world.

Pardee's struggling just to get by. When I can, I stop in and—"

"Will you get on with it?" Dixon asked impatiently.

Cooney gave him an injured look. "I'd run out of sugar, so I stopped in at Quincy's. I thought it funny that the front door was wide open."

Dixon sighed. He was going to have to let Cooney tell this his own way.

"I yelled Pardee's name a couple of times, then I got this funny feeling. It was like he was still there, but he couldn't talk."

Steve saw the congesting color in Dixon's face. He wasn't going to stand much more of this long drawn-out story.

"So I started looking for him," Cooney went on. This was an important moment in his life, and he was milking it for all he could get.

"I looked behind the counter, and there was old Pardee. Deader than a mackerel."

A hollow sigh escaped Steve. This was one of those nights, the kind that would never end.

"He was shot," Dixon stated.

Cooney stared astounded at him. "How did you know that?"

"It just figured, Billy. We've had some really bad characters running loose tonight. Could you tell if anything had been taken?"

"I didn't take time to look around. I just tore after you as fast as I could."

"There's another one for you to pick up, Andrews," Dixon said, turning his head toward the undertaker.

Andrews made a frightened little bleat. "Will this ever stop?"

"It'd better," Dixon said with a cynical smile. "Or we'll run out of people."

He headed for the door, Cooney and Steve at his heels. That game leg was wearying, and after a short burst of speed, Dixon was limping again.

Steve and Cooney caught up with him. "Do you think you know who did it, Marshal?"

"I could make a good guess."

"The Divens gang," Steve burst out.

Dixon nodded. "It all ties in. First, Jake at the jail, Babcock at the livery stable, now Quincy at the grocery store. Every time, they got something they need. First, their freedom; next, horses; last, supplies. Notice they picked an out-of-the-way store?"

Steve nodded grimly. Everything fit.

Not a word passed among the three until they reached Quincy's store. Dixon paused to scan the ground before the tie rail.

"Horses been here," he announced. "They did quite a bit of stomping around. I can't make out how many there were. But more than one." He stared at the store, and his expression was grim. "We might as well go in."

Steve and Cooney followed Dixon into the store. Dixon headed straight for the counter. He went around the end and stared frozenly at the pitiful figure on the floor. Quincy had died hard. His expression was a mixture of horror and pain.

"Those murdering bastards," Dixon said savagely. "Here's another one of the helpless ones."

Steve nodded. Dixon was lumping Jake, Babcock, and Quincy in the same category.

"What's our next move, Sam?"

"They'll be heading for Hell's Fringe as fast as they can get there. The local law won't want to follow them in. I'll round up a few of our deputies and take after them." His hand closed into a hard fist. "God, how I want to get my hands on them."

A thought occurred to Steve, and he shook his head.

"What's eating on you?" Dixon asked crossly.

Steve didn't want to tell Dixon what was wracking him. Dixon had a sixteen-year-old daughter. She had been motherless since she was five years old, and Dixon had done a creditable job of raising her. She and Dixon lived on a ten acre plot, some twelve miles out of town. Steve had been out there many times. All those threats Divens had made against Dixon hammered inside Steve's skull. Would Divens try to hurt Dixon through Sally? He groaned hollowly at the thought. As crazed as Divens was, it was entirely possible.

"Spit it out," Dixon said passionately.

Steve sighed. "Sam, I just happened to think of Sally. Do you think Divens would go after her?"

Dixon's jaw muscles bunched as he stared at Steve. The moonlight was strong enough for Steve to see his face had turned ashen. "Steve, are you suggesting—" He choked and couldn't finish.

"I'm only saying it could be possible," Steve answered gravely. "Charley Divens made a lot of threats against you. With that twisted mind, he could do anything to get even."

"Oh God," Dixon moaned. "Steve, get out there as fast as you can. Take my horse. You'll be able to make better time without me."

Steve briefly closed his eyes as he thought of Sally. She was a tremendous help to Dixon. She had a spitfire manner, and she and Steve did a lot of jawing at each other. He wasn't in love with her, but he had a tremendous fondness for her. The thought of Divens stopping out there made Steve sick to his stomach.

"Hurry," Dixon begged. "I won't be able to draw a free breath until you return."

"I'm on my way, Sam." Steve broke into a run toward the marshal's office. He wanted to pick up his rifle. He was glad he would have Dixon's horse. His own horse was a poor plug by comparison.

CHAPTER 8

PARNELL kicked his horse into faster motion and caught up with Charley and Elmer. "Hey," Parnell complained, his face showing alarm, "we're not heading for the Fringe."

"Odie's getting brighter," Charley said maliciously. "He can tell which way his nose is headed."

Elmer went into a paroxysm of mirth, slapping his thigh. Charley could always tickle him.

"Don't I have a right to know where we're headed?" Parnell asked sullenly.

"I told you back in town we had one more stop to make

before we ride for the Fringe. It won't take more than a few minutes."

"We're going to have the whole town on our tails," Parnell muttered, resisting the temptation to look back. Charley would give him hell if he caught him looking back. "I'm telling you we'd better keep moving," Parnell said definitely. "After what we did back there."

"Oh for God's sake," Charley howled. "The only one they can pin on us is Jake. Nobody knows we stopped at Babcock's stable or Quincy's store."

Parnell's resistance faded under Charley's fierce glare. "Can I ask where we're headed?"

"Sure." Charley grinned at the thought of how Odie would react when he heard where the spot was. "Marshal Dixon's house."

Parnell couldn't suppress the bleat of terror. Charley must be completely out of his mind.

"No, Charley," he said in a faltering voice.

"I'm running this affair," Charley snarled. "Elmer agrees with what I say. You can cut out if you don't like it."

Unconsciously, Parnell shivered. He didn't want to stay with the Divens, and he didn't want to be alone. His voice went flat. "Do you know where the marshal's place is?"

"I know." The confidence was big in Charley's voice. "I know he's got a daughter out there." Those piercing eyes dared Parnell to make a comment.

"Oh my God," Parnell moaned. "You touch her, and Dixon will tear you apart, a piece at a time."

"You're overlooking one thing," Charley said sarcastically. "He's got to catch us first. I promised at the jail I'd get even with him. He started all this. I'll give him something he'll never forget."

Parnell shook his head, but he didn't comment. He sat rigidly in the saddle, and his face was strained.

Charley halted them with an outthrust arm. "There it is," he announced.

Moonlight bathed the small house. The scene looked peaceful. No evil seemed to threaten it.

"I don't see no lights," Charley said. "She's gone to bed. Ain't she gonna be surprised when she sees who wakes her?"

Parnell's mouth was so dry he couldn't swallow. When he tried to speak, only a squeak came out of him. Molest-

ing a woman was the worst crime of all. That would
arouse all the animal savagery in a man.

He tried again, and a small sound came out. "There
should be a dog around here. His barking might arouse
her."

"I'm getting sick and tired of all your objections,"
Charley hissed. "We'll ride around the house and check
things out."

A complete round of the house revealed nothing. Every
window in the house was dark. "There ain't nothing to
stop us," Charley said with immense satisfaction. "Everything is going our way."

Parnell didn't dare let his moan be heard. What Charley
had in mind was bad. Parnell felt cold and clammy. He
was sweating and cold at the same time.

"We going in through the front door, Charley?" Elmer
asked.

"It'll probably be locked. We'll see if a window is open.
If we have to, we can try the front door."

They tethered their horses a hundred yards from the
house. Parnell sweated harder, and his skin was clammier
as they crawled up to the house. They wouldn't last ten
seconds, if anybody saw them.

Charley worked around the house, trying each window
as he came to it. His face grew angrier as he found each
one locked. He tried the kitchen window last, and it
squeaked as it rose a couple of inches.

His face went taut, and he pulled his hands away and
waited. "Nobody heard that," he whispered, an exultant
ring in his voice. "I'll take it slower." He raised the window a fraction of an inch at a time. It took a disturbingly
long time to raise the window, but there were no squeals
from it. If there was any sound, it was only a sigh, a rustle
of sound. He turned a triumphant face toward Parnell. Let
him comment on that.

Parnell's face was drawn tight. If somebody found them
in here, they wouldn't survive long; only long enough to
meet a hang rope.

The three climbed in through the window, and Charley
looked around the room. He saw the well-stocked pantry
shelves and hissed, "Hell, we could have got everything we
want here." A vagrant moonlight glistened on the blade of
a butcher knife. He picked it up and held it in his hand.
There was no telling when a knife would come in handy.

They prowled through two rooms, and they were empty. "This one has to be her bedroom," Charley whispered. He motioned the two to remain outside the door. "I'll check it out."

Sally had never fully gotten back to sleep after the first noise. She tossed restlessly, whimpering deep in her throat. She sensed something evil in this room.

Her eyes flew open in terror as something cold touched her throat. She tried to sit up, and a hand shoved her back roughly.

"One sound," a voice hissed, "and I'll cut your throat."

She lay back, her eyes wide. This was no bad dream; a man was in her room. She couldn't make out his features. He was only a dark blob beside her bed.

She had to moisten her lips before she could speak. "What do you want?" she gasped.

"You," a brutal voice said. The knife blade bore harder against her throat, and she shrank under its touch. "Scream, and it'll be your last."

Sally's senses were reeling, and she struggled frantically to hang onto them. "If it's money you want, I haven't got much. But I'll give you what I have."

The shadowy figure laughed coarsely. "You haven't got enough money to buy yourself out of this. Get up and get dressed."

Sally was beginning to shake, and her teeth clicked as she tried to speak. "Where are you taking me?"

"Why don't you come along and see?" A hand seized the blanket covering her and ripped it away. "I told you to get dressed. I won't tell you again."

"I'm not dressing with you in the room," she said indignantly.

That coarse laughter rang out again. "You're going to learn quite a few things before you're through."

Hang on, she kept advising herself. You're dealing with a madman. Do as he says.

"I can't dress with you here," she said hollowly.

The snicker scraped across her skin. "You'll get used to a lot worse before this is over."

Sally fought off the encroaching terror. She had to do as he said; she had to buy time. She crawled out of bed and turned her back on him. She still felt his eyes boring into her.

She gathered up her clothes before she stripped off the nightgown. Humiliation filled her, making her skin burn.

"My papa will kill you for this," she said in a shaking voice.

"He won't do a damned thing," the man assured her.

She reached for her undergarments, and he snapped, "Don't waste time with all that female frippery. The dress is enough unless you want to go like you are."

Inner sobs shook her body as she pulled the dress over her head. "Can I put on my boots?" she wailed.

"Put them on. But don't try anything else."

He waited until she tugged on her boots, then grabbed her arm and hurried her out of the room. Her terror spread as she saw the other two. My God, this was a nightmare and growing.

"Unlock the door," the voice behind her said. An arm extended over her shoulder, and the blade was still close to her throat.

"Remember what I said about screaming," the voice said.

Sally drew a deep breath to stop the shaking. She had to go along until she saw some opportunity to escape these men.

Charley marched her to where the horses were tethered. "Climb up," he ordered.

His rage grew at her hesitation. "You're going to learn it's smart to do what I say. Oh you're going to learn a lot."

Rough hands seized her at the waist and hoisted her into the saddle. Sally thought she was going to be thrown clear over the animal. Her arms flailed, and she grasped frantically for something to hold onto. One hand caught the reins and stopped her slide down the other side of the horse.

Charley bounded up behind her, and he reached out and steadied her. One arm went around her waist, and the fingers bit into her flesh. The other hand held the knife, and its point pricked her side.

"If we happen to see anybody, this is to warn you what would happen if you scream."

Charley turned his head toward the other two. "I'll hold her here, while you two go back in and take anything you want from the pantry."

Sally waited until the two other men went into the

house. She bit her lip to keep the quaver out of her voice. "You're going to regret this. My father is Marshal Dixon."

Charley chuckled. "Is that so? Why do you think I picked you out? Your father got me sent to jail. I swore I'd get even with him. Maybe I'll send you back to him when I get through with you and maybe not. Depends on a lot of things." He kept up that evil chuckling.

Sally kept her lips clamped tight to block the screams that threatened to burst out.

Elmer and Parnell came back out. Elmer carried another gunny bag. "Filled it up, Charley," Elmer said.

"Good. Let's ride."

Sally's eyes were blinded with tears. She didn't know where they were going. Perhaps it was best that she didn't.

CHAPTER 9

STEVE drove Dixon's horse as hard as he dared, stopping every now and then to give the animal a breather. He couldn't risk having the horse drop dead before they reached Dixon's house. He fretted away those brief respites. Each time, he waited until the sweating lessened on the horse before he urged it on.

All the things he should have taken kept running through his mind. He didn't dare spend a lot of time gathering them. He had a picket rope in the saddlebags and a blanket. He hadn't stopped to gather up supplies. Besides, at this hour most of the grocery stores were closed.

His chest hurt with anxiety as he finally came in sight of the house. It looked peaceful in the moonlight. Steve couldn't explain the uneasy feeling that knotted his guts. He rode up to the house and swung off. The front door standing open was like a kick in the belly. Sally would never have been careless enough to go off and leave the door open.

"Sally," he called. The silence mocked him. He entered the house, calling her name repeatedly. His only answer was an echo that told him nothing. There was a terrible mess in the kitchen. The shelves were stripped, and cans were scattered aimlessly about on the floor. Sally was a meticulous housekeeper. She would never let her kitchen get so disorderly. Somebody had ransacked these shelves.

He would look through the rest of the house, but he knew it would do no good. No, somebody had abducted Sally, and Steve could easily put names to them. Charley Divens and his two followers. So far, Charley had made his threat of revenge against Dixon too true.

Steve searched through the bedroom. He saw no great signs of disorder, but the rumpled bed told him too much. Sally would never leave a bed in this shape.

His mouth was a thin, bitter line as he re-entered the kitchen. Sally was gone, and he was afraid he couldn't catch up with Charley before physical harm was done to her. He knew Dixon would be waiting anxiously for his return. Dixon had taken a place far out of town to keep Sally away from the kind of scum that infested the cities and towns. It hadn't done much good. Steve muttered a string of oaths. He knew how badly Dixon wanted to hear from him, but he couldn't afford the time to return to Oklahoma City and tell him what had happened. He had to pick up the tracks right now and keep on them until he ran Divens and the other two to ground. The waiting would distress Dixon, but Steve could see no other way.

He found a small, empty sack and filled it with assorted cans. He hoped it would be enough to carry him as far as he had to go. He looked into the small shed behind the house before he left. Sally's pony was there. That was final proof that she had been taken under duress. Steve untied the pony, led it outside and whacked it on the rump. He watched it disappear. The pony would have to fend for it- self until Steve found time to return.

He picked up the tracks immediately. It had rained less than a week ago, and the ground retained prints well. But tracking at night was a slow and tedious business. Steve kept at it until his eyes were too heavy to continue farther.

He almost fell out of the saddle, and stumbling, he led the horse to a nearby creek. Fighting the need for sleep was a cruel business, and he thought he would fall asleep while waiting for the horse to finish drinking.

"Come on," he said hoarsely. That damned horse was taking an inordinate amount of time. Instead of drinking and getting it over with, the animal played with the water, thrusting its muzzle into the stream and blowing great bubbles.

"That's got to do you for now," Steve muttered, yanking on the reins.

The horse came out of the stream reluctantly, resisting Steve every step of the way. Steve literally hauled the animal over to a small clump of trees. He strung his picket line between two of them. The grass was good here, and that would have to do until he grabbed a few winks.

He stretched out near the horse and was instantly asleep. He didn't see the first, faint dawn. Complete exhaustion held him until the rising sun played full on his face.

Steve groaned as he returned foggily to consciousness. He would guess that he hadn't slept more than a couple of hours, and it wasn't enough to revive him. Every muscle ached, and he felt as though he had been trampled on by a stampeding herd.

He walked to the stream, dipped his face into the water and drank until he was filled. He raised his head out of the water, shook the drops from it, then splashed handfuls of water into his face. He felt better. Maybe only half of that herd had trampled him.

God, he wanted a cup of coffee. Two things prevented that. First, he had no coffee, and there wasn't time to build a fire and wait for the coffee to boil even if he did. No, he would have to do with a can he had taken from Sally's larder.

He jabbed the point of a hunting knife into a can of tomatoes, then sawed the remainder of the lid away. He tilted the can and drank from its contents. Without salt, it tasted flat, but he wasn't complaining. He slapped his stomach when he finished. It wasn't the most elaborate meal in the world, but it would hold him.

Steve walked down to the stream and drank, then sloshed more water into his face. He moved back to the horse. In the radius of the rein's reach, it had cropped the grass down to the earth. It probably wasn't enough, but for the time being, it would have to do.

"Come on, boy," Steve growled. "We've got some important work to do."

He bit back an oath as he hoisted himself into the saddle. That brief sleep hadn't refreshed him. He ached in every bone.

He picked up the trail immediately, and he could proceed at a far faster clip, only glancing at the tracks now and then to be sure he hadn't strayed. He passed a couple of small towns, but he didn't stop to ask for information. Steve doubted that Divens would go near a town with his prisoner.

Steve's eyes sharpened as the tracks turned abruptly to the west. "He's heading for Hell's Fringe," he muttered. It didn't surprise him. He was sure that had been Divens' destination from the start. Only lawbreakers entered Hell's Fringe, and once Steve was in the strip, he wouldn't find a friendly person. Lawbreakers looked with disfavor on a lawman who attempted to follow them.

If Divens continued in this direction, he would come out somewhere in Kiowa, Comanche and Apache land. Steve doubted that Divens would go into Indian land. No, he would stop somewhere in Hell's Fringe. Steve didn't know exactly where. Poor Sally, he thought. It would take time to find her. She must be going through hell right now. But the thin strip narrowed down the search considerably, even it if ran a long way. Steve sighed at the difficulties ahead of him. Divens had a long lead on him, and it was going to take time to whittle it away. Steve's face was harsh and foreboding as he thought of an anxiously waiting Dixon.

CHAPTER 10

SALLY sagged in the saddle. Only Charley's arms kept her from falling. It had been a long, hard ride, draining her physically and emotionally. She knew the morning of the first day, who had taken her. She had turned her head to plead further with him, and the disfiguring pigment on his left cheek pulled a startled gasp out of her. "You're Charley Divens, aren't you?" she stammered.

He grinned with evil enjoyment. "So you know me, huh? I suppose your old man talked about me."

"No," she denied faintly and said nothing more. But her terror was increasing. Sam had talked about Divens and his crimes. He even mentioned Divens' threat of getting even.

"Doesn't it worry you?" she asked.

"Ninety per cent of them squeal like trapped rats when they're caught," Dixon had answered. "If I allowed myself to fret over all the threats I've received, I would never know a decent night's sleep."

"Maybe you should start being concerned," she had replied.

"As long as I wear this badge, I won't worry, Sally. I've got a job to do. When I start worrying about myself, the job won't get done."

Sam meant what he said, she thought dully. He was worrying now. She writhed inwardly from anguish. What could he do about it? What could she do? Divens was striking back at her father through her. All during the long ride, she had thought of a hundred ways to escape this wicked man. But Divens had never diverted his attention from her, even in the short rest periods.

Tears oozed from her eyes, and she couldn't stop them. She wanted to scream and rave, but she couldn't let this monster see her distress. It would only amuse him. Papa, she thought, I won't disgrace you.

It was getting close to evening, for the sun was low on the horizon. "Maybe that's what we're looking for," Charley said. He pointed at the dilapidated hovel just up ahead. The strip was filled with such sad shelters. None of them was occupied for very long. Any man who fled into the Fringe was never content to rest long. "It looks deserted," Charley commented.

"Not much of a place," Parnell observed.

Charley turned an angry face toward him. "What did you expect, a fine hotel? It'll do for us. Let's see if it's occupied."

The horses moved up to the shack. Charley hailed the shack. "Anybody here?" He flashed a triumphant grin at his two companions. "Looks like it's empty." He slid to the ground and held up his arms to Sally. "Come on. Get down."

Sheer terror held her. Whatever was in store for her would happen here. She shook her head.

Charley grabbed her hand. "You're gonna learn to do what I tell you." He yanked on her arm, pulling her off the horse. Only his rough hands prevented her from falling. She was so stiff and sore she didn't think she could move.

Charley gripped her hand and pulled her into the shack. It had been a long time since this place was used, for a thick coat of dust was over everything. A stove, a table, and three chairs were the only items of furniture, and everything was much the worse for use.

"Whoever had this place didn't leave much, or have much to start with," Elmer commented. He looked up at the roof, where faint streaks of light came through. "Hell," he said in disgust, "it ain't even got a decent roof on it."

"It ain't raining now, is it?" Charley snarled. He pushed Sally toward a room. The hinges squeaked dismally as the door was opened.

This room was even more poorly furnished than the kitchen. A rusty iron bed with a sad-looking mattress were the only items in the room.

"Just what I was looking for," Charley said, baring his teeth in a vicious grin. "Here's where I start getting even." He pushed Sally into the room, then turned to block Elmer and Parnell from entering. "I'm going to be busy for a while. Go out and rustle up some firewood. You want supper, don't you?"

"We sure do," Elmer replied. He winked at Charley and walked toward the front door.

Charley closed the door, and the hinges creaked dolorously.

Sally shrank back into a corner, her eyes enormous in a pale face. "What are you going to do?" She stammered so badly that her teeth chattered.

Charley advanced a slow step at a time. "Why, I'm going to teach you how to become a woman."

Elmer and Parnell came back into the shack with armfuls of dried wood. They didn't have to go far. A fair-sized tree just outside of the shack had died and gone down, breaking off a great number of its limbs. It was a simple matter to pick up pieces of the limbs.

They dropped their armloads onto the floor beside the stove. Elmer turned his head toward the closed door. "Wonder what's going on in there?"

Parnell worriedly shook his head. "I got a bad feeling about this, Elmer. This could bring us a lot of trouble."

"Shut up," Elmer said in disgust. He glared at Parnell. He was beginning to appreciate how Charley felt about Parnell.

A sudden, shrill scream rang out, coming clearly through the closed door.

"What was that?" a startled Parnell asked.

"You sure don't know very much," Elmer said disdainfully. "I'd say old Charley just cut himself a prize hog."

CHAPTER 11

SALLY lay on her back, her eyes closed. She breathed shallowly, afraid that even breathing would increase the pain. She was bruised of body and soul. God, if there was only some way she could kill this monster.

"Come on. Get up," Charley ordered. "The boys must be getting hungry by now. I want you to fix our supper."

"I haven't got any pots or pans," she said.

Charley grinned at her. "Plumb forgot to bring any. Just heat up the cans. That'll do."

"How do I open them?" she asked helplessly.

"You sure can't fend for yourself," Charley said, but he didn't sound too unhappy. He pulled the butcher knife from his belt. "Guess you never had to do with make-shifts." He jabbed the point of the knife into eight or nine lids. "You can saw the lids open, can't you?"

"Yes," she said meekly. Her pulses were throbbing so hard she was afraid he would notice it. If he only turned away, leaving the knife here, perhaps she could hide it under the oversized shirt sleeve. If she could get the knife into the bedroom without being noticed, her opportunity would come. She would make sure of that.

She laid the fire, and Charley supplied the match. "After we eat, maybe we'll pick up the good time," he whispered.

"Maybe," she murmured, looking shyly at him.

"Hey," he said in obvious delight, "you turned into a woman quicker than I expected."

She heated the cans and set them on the table. She came back after the last can and slipped the knife up a sleeve, holding the haft in her palm. The sleeve was long enough to completely hide the knife.

She started to move toward the bedroom, and Charley

cried, "You haven't eaten anything. Come here and sit by me."

Her heart pounded so that she was afraid it would shake her body. She kept a smooth, expressionless face and said, "I'm too excited to eat. I'll be waiting for you."

Elmer slapped his leg and guffawed. "Charley, you really knock them over."

"It's all in knowing how," Charley said and winked.

He stood, and Elmer said, "Hey, you haven't eaten much."

"A man gets a lot of different hungers in his head," Charley winked again. "He takes care of the most important one first." He sauntered toward the bedroom door.

Sally had checked out which way the door swung open. She wasn't going to let a mishap mar her opportunity. She had pushed back the sleeve and held the knife firmly in her hand. A chance at one savage thrust was all she wanted. She would be behind the door when it swung open.

She stiffened as she heard the approaching footsteps. Her heart beat so fiercely she was certain it would pound its way out of her breast.

The door swung open, shielding her. Charley stepped into the room.

"Hey," he called. "Where are you?" He shut the door, and she was behind him.

"Right behind you," Sally said softly.

Charley turned, the beginning of a grin on his face. The grin disappeared, to be replaced by horror as he saw the knife in her hand.

"Wait a minute," he gasped. "Didn't I—"

"You did," she said coldly. She stepped forward, covering the distance between them. She drove the knife forward with all her strength.

Charley tried to block the thrust with a sweep of his arm, but the shock of seeing her standing there with a knife had numbed his mind, blocking his physical reaction. His arm was too late to do more than brush her hand.

The momentum of her arm was sufficient to drive the knife into his belly up to the haft. He moaned softly, and his eyes bulged. His lips pulled back in a ghastly grimace that gave him a death's-head appearance. He staggered back a step, his weight pulling the knife from her hand.

She cowered, thinking surely he would try to reach her. He stared at her with those dreadful, bulging eyes. He tried to pull the knife from his belly, but the strength wasn't in him. He could, however, manage the fading strength to take a few, dragging steps. His hands were clasped about the haft of the knife, and blood spurted between his fingers.

Sally watched every movement he made with fascinated eyes. She knew no remorse, only a jubilant triumph. She had seen her opportunity and used it well.

Charley had trouble getting the door open. He fought it until it was open enough for him to stagger through. He took a step into the kitchen, and he was beginning to falter.

Elmer and Parnell heard his entrance, and both whirled in their chairs. For a moment, neither saw the bloody hands gripping the knife, but Charley's expression told them that something bad had happened.

"Charley," Elmer started, "what the hell?"

Charley had trouble speaking. His lips moved feebly, and his voice was only a thin reed of sound. "That goddamn woman stabbed me," he managed. His eyes rolled up into his head, and he pitched forward on his face.

CHAPTER 12

ELMER sprang to his feet and rushed to where Charley lay. Elmer dropped onto his knees and turned the dying man over.

"Why, Charley?" he begged.

Charley tried to speak, but a rush of blood into his mouth blotted out the words. The light in his eyes was fading, and his breathing was becoming more labored.

Tears filled Elmer's eyes as he watched his brother die. Parnell was still frozen to his chair, his face stupid with horror.

A voice turned Elmer's head. "I'm damned glad I did

it," Sally said. She was on the verge of hysteria. "I wish I could do it a dozen times over."

Elmer saw the blood, Charley's blood, on the shirt she wore. The sight of blood on her right hand broke his last restraint. He and Charley had been close ever since they were kids. Charley had always looked out for him and protected him. Fragments of remembered pictures flashed through his mind. There was the woman who had killed Charley. Elmer didn't give a damn why; only the fact that she was there blotted out all reason.

The shotgun taken from Babcock's stable leaned in a corner. Elmer had never unloaded it. He sprang to his feet, snatched it up and whirled.

"You damned murderer!" he shouted. He cocked the hammer as he spoke and pulled the trigger. He was only a few feet from Sally, and the blast of the gun literally blew her into the other room.

Elmer didn't go into the room to see if she was dead. At that range, there was no other possibility.

Parnell shook as though he had the ague. "Oh my God," he moaned. "Now you've done it."

Elmer stared at him like a madman. It was fortunate that the shotgun was a single-barreled weapon, or Elmer might have pulled the trigger again.

"Elmer," Parnell pleaded, throwing up supplicating hands, "it's Odie."

Sanity returned to Elmer's eyes, and he lowered the weapon. He could barely control the shaking of his hands. "She deserved it," he said, squinching his eyes to keep tears from spilling out. "She killed Charley."

She had every right to do it, Parnell thought. But he was wise enough not to express the thought. "We've got to get out of here," he said frantically. "They'll really be after us now." Killing a woman was the worst crime a man could commit. Everybody in the territory would be in full bay after them.

"Not until we bury Charley," Elmer said through clenched teeth.

"My God," Parnell demurred, "we can't afford the time. We've got to get going—" He fell silent at the animal savagery in Elmer's face.

"We bury him," Elmer said, pacing the floor. "But we can't do it until morning."

An invisible hand seemed to clutch Parnell by the

throat, making it difficult to breathe. This was a foolish decision, and he wanted to protest against it. Another look at Elmer dried up the protest. Elmer was crazy wild with grief. There was no telling what he would do. "Can we start early in the morning, Elmer?" he begged.

Elmer nodded mutely. He stared at something only he could see.

Parnell wanted to start at dawn, but Elmer said, "Not light enough yet. Goddamn it," he raved. "Will you ease down? We're too far ahead for them to catch up with us." He had spent a bad night. Sleep wouldn't come, and he rolled and tossed. Every time he turned the right way, he saw Charley's body. In some way Elmer couldn't explain, it seemed to be accusing him. "I couldn't stop it, Charley," he whispered. "How did I know she was going to do that?" He pounded a fist against the floor. If this grief didn't ease, it was going to drive him out of his mind.

He dragged himself to his feet when the light strengthened. He knew a fierce resentment at the steady volume of Parnell's snoring. Parnell had apparently rested well. He didn't have grief keeping him awake. For an instant, Elmer knew an almost uncontrollable rage against him. Elmer put a hard grip on his feeling and shook Parnell awake. He might need Parnell before they were out of this. "Wake up," he said harshly. "Time to get to work."

"Ain't we going to eat something first?" Parnell complained.

Elmer shrugged. "I'm not hungry. There's some unopened cans over there. Help yourself."

Rage flickered in his eyes as he watched Parnell use the same knife to open a few cans, the knife that had killed Charley. To keep from an outbreak Elmer said, "Hurry it up. I'll be waiting for you outside."

He walked around the house, trying to pick a site for the grave. This was a barren, desolate land. He couldn't find even a tree, or a sturdy bush under which to bury Charley. His hands clenched until they ached. Oh God, there was no possible way of making a coffin. For an instant, he thought of trying to rip off some of the boards of the house. He tentatively tried a few, and they broke and splintered in his hands. He did keep a couple of pieces. They would have to do in place of a shovel.

Parnell came out, and Elmer resented his belching. Charley, lying dead in there, didn't mean a thing to him.

Elmer tossed him one of the boards. "Get to digging," he said curtly.

"With this?" Parnell squalled. "It'll never take the place of a shovel."

"Then use your hands," Elmer said unfeelingly. "We're not going to leave here until Charley's properly buried."

Parnell kept his grumbling to himself. Grief had pushed Elmer to his limit.

Fortunately, the ground was softened by recent rain, but at best, this was a torturously slow job.

Parnell worked a good three hours. The sun slowly rose, and the sweat stains on his shirt grew. Parnell's back ached, and he had blisters on his hands. He wanted to quit, he wanted to yell his resentment, but he didn't dare. Every time he slowed to take a breath, those burning eyes bored into him.

He straightened to ease his back. "I can't dig any deeper," he said sullenly. "The ground's too damned hard." Twice in the past few moments the board had broken.

Elmer looked wildly at the hole. They were down below the rain-softened earth, and he couldn't disagree with Parnell. He had tried using his hands, and the nails were broken and his fingers bleeding.

Elmer threw the board from Parnell in savage rage. Elmer guessed the hole to be less than two feet deep. It wasn't nearly what he wanted, but it would have to do.

"All right," he said grudgingly and climbed out of the hole. Parnell's loud sigh of relief further infuriated him. "Let's carry him out." If he wasn't able to keep his temper under control, he didn't know what would happen. He and Parnell weren't out of this by a long way, and Elmer might need him.

Elmer groaned as they walked into the house.

"What is it?" Parnell cried. He was sure jumpy this morning. Any little alien sound could upset him.

"I just thought of something," Elmer answered. "We don't have a blanket, and there wasn't any in the house."

Parnell nodded in agreement, though he didn't see why it was so important.

"You dummy," Elmer railed at him. "Do you think I want to throw dirt in Charley's face?"

Parnell shrugged. Charley was dead. It wouldn't matter

to him. He remained silent, wisely knowing that any word could set Elmer off.

Elmer's eyes briefly touched his brother's face before he could jerk them away. Charley looked awful. His face was beginning to blacken, and the flesh had stiffened until it no longer looked like a human face. Elmer closed his eyes. That brief glimpse made him more determined than ever. He would not throw dirt in that unprotected face.

He thought of something, and his eyes burned. That woman had been wearing a dress when she entered the room with Charley. She hadn't been wearing it when she came out. The dress should still be in the other room.

He tried to avoid looking, but he caught a vague glimpse of her. She lay huddled on her side where she had fallen after he shot her. He saw the dress on the floor in a far corner. He picked it up and hurried out.

"What about her?" Parnell asked.

"What do you mean?" Elmer asked fiercely.

"You're not just going to leave her there," Parnell protested.

"The hell I'm not," Elmer shouted. "That bitch killed Charley."

Parnell's hands clenched. He had never seen such an unforgiving streak in a man. Maybe it was only proof of how much Elmer cared for his brother.

"Take his feet," Elmer ordered. He stooped to pick up Charley's body by the shoulders.

Charley's body was stiff and awkward to handle. Parnell caught one of the feet in the doorway. He was sweating hard, and he cast a harried glance at Elmer. Elmer would jump all over him for that.

Elmer's eyes flashed furious accusations at Parnell, but he didn't say anything.

Together, they placed Charley in the open grave. Elmer stood there a long moment looking down. He didn't cry, but his face was too rigid. He must be crying inwardly. Finally, he bent over and placed the ruined dress over Charley's face. He straightened and seemed to be seeking something to say.

He looked up at the sky. "Oh God, take care of him. He wasn't all bad."

Parnell wanted to snort. Charley was mostly bad. But he didn't dare say that.

Elmer kept up that silent communication a long moment, then said harshly, "All right. Fill it up."

Parnell scraped his boot against the piled-up dirt, and a small stream cascaded into the grave.

"Not that way," Elmer said weakly.

"There's no shovel," Parnell said weakly.

"You've got your hands," Elmer snapped. He kneeled beside the grave and let two handfuls of dirt trickle across the cloth over Charley's face.

Parnell sighed and kneeled on the other side. This was going to take forever.

Charley had been a hard taskmaster. Parnell wondered if Elmer would be the same, now that he had the authority. Parnell sighed. Several times in the past he wished he had never thrown in with the Divens boys. Now the feeling was stronger than ever.

CHAPTER 13

STEVE rode doggedly, trying to ignore the discomforts that plagued him. He was galled, and every muscle in his body ached. He had less than four hours' sleep in the past twenty-four hours, and he was running short of food.

He wondered how far he was behind his quarry. He had lost the tracks yesterday after crossing a stretch of rocky soil. He had to backtrack until he found a small rock that looked as though it had been kicked out of the earth by a hoof. Steve dismounted and fingered the soil about the edge of the hole where the rock had been. It felt fairly fresh. If this put him back on the trail, he couldn't be too far behind them.

He grunted as he climbed back into the saddle. He still had to guess as to the right direction to head. A slight scuff mark wouldn't point out anything to him, except that horses had passed this way. God, let him have a little luck. The thought of all that lost time was gnawing away at him.

The rocky stretch ran out, and it didn't take much searching for Steve to pick up the tracks again. Maybe he could make up a little of the lost time.

The sun was almost overhead when he caught a glimpse of a shack at least a half mile ahead. He pulled up and sat studying the structure. It looked lonely and desolate from here, as though it hadn't been lived in for quite a while. But he could not pass it by without investigating.

He slid down and pulled the rifle out of its scabbard. He used the picket line to put the horse on a long tether. The grass wasn't too good here, but there should be enough to hold him. He swore at the absence of timber around the shack. It would make it difficult to approach without being observed.

He found a swag in the ground that would give some protection. He dropped to his hands and knees and crawled along it, every now and then raising his head to check his progress. The air of silence about the house held, but those tracks had pointed in this direction.

The swag bent a little to the east of the house, but Steve still clung to it. He could get closer by remaining with this protection, then trying to gain time by directly approaching the building.

The swag ran out, and Steve risked another glimpse. He judged he was some sixty yards from the shack, and he debated upon his course. Setting his teeth hard, he crawled out and, holding his rifle across his arms, crawled as close to the ground as he could. In twenty yards, he was bathed in sweat, and it wasn't due to physical exertion, but anticipation of being the object of a few well-aimed bullets.

He kept edging closer. If somebody was in that shack, he had to be asleep not to have seen his approach. Some thirty yards from the house Steve passed a long, narrow mound of freshly turned dirt. By its size and shape, it could be nothing but a grave.

Steve pondered over whose it was. He got to his feet and brushed the dirt off his clothes. He felt quite certain the house was no longer occupied. But it had been once; the grave testified to that. Was it one of the three he was after? He could only presume it was.

He walked toward the shack, the rifle in one hand, the

pistol ready in his right. He paused at the doorway, listening for alien sound. He heard nothing but silence, and it had a mournful quality.

Bounding through the door, he threw himself up against a wall. The creaking protest of the boards was the only sound, and Steve waited while his heart settled down.

His original instincts were valid. The shack was unoccupied. He moved about the kitchen, opening the stove door and looking into it. A fire had been built in here, and he felt the ashes to see if he could determine when. The ashes felt warm, but that could have been due to his imagination. He felt no embers or any actual heat. He looked at the emptied cans on the floor. Those three had been here sometime last night.

He headed for the door of the other room. He opened it, and it creaked dolorously. Then he saw Sally. His heart jumped into his throat, and his breathing almost stopped.

"Oh God," he cried. Sally was on her side, and the stillness of her form told him everything before he made a closer inspection.

Steve was frozen for a long moment, a hundred remembered scenes flashing through his mind. Sally had been a little spitfire, laughing one moment, quiet the next. But the reflection that hit him the hardest was of an anxious father waiting for news.

He moved to the pitiful, huddled figure. The damned flies were everywhere, and he yanked off his hat and slashed furiously at them. They rose in a buzzing, angry cloud, then came back.

Gently, he turned Sally over. The tears stung his eyes as he looked at that poor, mute face. She was dressed only in a soiled shirt, and there were numerous blood stains on it. He studied them intently. It wasn't hard to guess what had happened. Sally had been shot at close range with a shotgun. But why? That was the answer he had to have.

He straightened and looked at the miserable bed with its shabby mattress. He saw the dull, brown patches of blood at the door. Something ugly and violent had happened here. In some way had Sally revenged herself on her attacker? Maybe, he thought. The answer to that question might lay in that hastily dug grave outside. It might tell Steve who had attacked Sally and who killed her.

Steve hurried back to the tethered horse and pulled a rolled-up blanket from behind his saddle. There was an urgency in his motions that made him pant. He couldn't stand the thought of those filthy flies crawling over Sally's face.

He placed the blanket over her, then walked slowly back to the grave. He kicked at the loose dirt, demolishing the mounded-up heap. From here on, he would have to use something other than his feet. He looked helplessly about for something with which to dig. He doubted there was a shovel or a tool of any kind around. He saw the two pieces of boards and the dirt-encrusted edges. Those boards had been used for digging. They would be poor substitutes for a shovel, but they would have to do.

He worked like a demented man, throwing out small showers of dirt. He was down to ground level, and he dropped the board, clawing away with his hands. The grave wasn't deep. It didn't take him long to uncover a figure. He clawed away the remaining dirt. A soiled, ripped dress covered the face. Steve recognized the material. That had once been a dress Sally had worn. Some of the answers were beginning to come to him.

Steve pulled the dress aside and stared down at the pigment-marked face. He was beginning to reconstruct the crime. Charley had been Sally's attacker, and in some way, she had managed to pay him back.

Elmer had placed her ruined dress over this figure's face to protect it from the dirt thrown into the grave. Steve knew how Elmer had revered his brother. Parnell might have helped, but under duress. He wouldn't have been concerned enough to think of this nicety.

Steve pulled the body out of the grave. Charley was bare to the waist, and that long, ugly wound in the belly told him what kind of a weapon had been used. It had to be a long, savage blade, a heavy knife such as a butcher knife. He sat on his heels, trying to rebuild the crime. It didn't save Sally, but he could exult in the fact that she had struck back. Elmer was the actual murderer. He had probably seen his brother stagger out of that bedroom, stumble a few steps, then slump. The blood stains on the floor attested to that surmise. Seeing his brother die had been more than enough to drive Elmer crazy. He had grabbed up a shotgun, probably the one taken from Babcock's stable, and emptied its charge into Sally.

Steve was unseeing as his eyes brimmed with tears. "You murdering bastard," he muttered. "I'll find you." In a sudden excess of fury, he bent over the grave and seized Charley by a shoulder. He pulled him free from the ground and dragged him a dozen yards away. He left the body lying there without another glance. He didn't give a damn what happened to it. Let the buzzards have the carcass.

He cleaned out the grave, and the hard-packed earth prevented him from digging it any deeper. He stared at the hole, shaking his head sorrowfully. He didn't want to leave Sally here, but it was the best he could do.

He walked back into the shack, picked up Sally, and carried her out to the grave. He carefully wrapped the blanket about her, then lowered her into the grave.

He stood there a long moment, thinking of something he could say, and nothing came to mind. "Sam will miss you, Sally," he said in a choking voice. "So will I." He stared up into the sky. "God, take care of her. She didn't ask for this."

He used a piece of board and scraped loose dirt into the grave. He worked in a kind of frenzy until he was bathed in sweat, and the moisture ran dirty runnels down his face.

He didn't have the slightest idea of how long it took, but he kept at it until he could no longer scrape up loose dirt to build the mound any higher. Even then, he wasn't satisfied. He scouted about the area, picking up any size stone he could find. He made several dozen trips, toting the stones back and placing them on the mound. He turned away, his shoulders slumping. That was the best he could do. He prayed those stones would keep predators from digging into the grave.

He walked back to the horse, untied its reins and mounted. "I don't know how long we'll be gone, boy," he said aloud. He was suddenly terribly lonely, and he needed the sound of a human voice. "Maybe a long time," he finished. He wouldn't stop until he caught up with those two.

It was easy to pick up the tracks of the three horses. By the depth of the tracks he figured two of them were being ridden while the third was led. Good, he thought bleakly. The led horse should slow them down some.

He rode through the day, quickening his pace when the tracks were clear and distinct. He prayed there would be an early moon, for he intended to keep on for most of the night. He shuddered at the thought of missing the tracks in the night and having to spend a lot of time finding them again.

As the time passed indeterminably, he finally stopped for a couple of hours' sleep near dawn. He hadn't realized he was so weary. The first step down from the saddle jerked a grunt out of him. His joints refused to work, and each movement was painful.

Steve walked about a bit, loosening up those stiffened joints. He picked a creek to stop by, and he drank until his belly rebelled. Water was going to have to do him, for he was down to a single can of food. He laved handfuls of water into his face, then ducked his head under the surface.

Before he fell asleep, he had been afraid his weariness would drag him down into deep, sodden slumber, running well into the coming day. He needn't have worried. A recurrent dream of Sally pleading with him for help kept jarring him awake.

He was up and saddling before the day's light was full and strong. God, he ached in every bone. That attempt at a brief rest had wrung him out worse than if he had kept on.

He cursed the empty, desolate country as he searched for the tracks again. The swearing dropped to an unhappy grumbling as he saw them. Were the tracks fresher, or was it only his imagination that was tormenting him?

A half-dozen times during the day he swung off to make a closer inspection of the tracks. He rubbed a pinch of dirt, taken from one of the tracks, between his thumb and forefinger. He could swear those grains of dirt were moist.

He kept his attention divided between the tracks and the horizon ahead of him. He didn't want to ride blindly into an ambush. These were hunted men and dangerous. They would cut down a pursuer and ask questions later.

He rode on steadily through the afternoon, holding down the impulse to demand more from his mount. He didn't want to burn it out before the objective he sought was in sight.

The sun was sinking low when Steve stiffened and reined up sharply. The sun was going down behind an obstacle on the horizon, and Steve studied it. Looking into the sun made his sight hazy, but that object had to be man-made.

He sat motionless until the sun sank and his eyes

weren't filled with the glare. It was a shack he was looking
at. Even at this distance, it was a desolate-looking place,
and there was an air of loneliness about it. Whoever had
built this place had probably moved on, abandoning it.
But it would be a welcome haven for two fleeing men. It
had to be checked out more closely, but Steve didn't want
to ride up to it now.

He rode back a half mile and tethered his horse to a
stubby bush. The grass here was sparse, and Steve shook
his head. It was a hell of a place to leave an animal. He
ran his hand down the horse's neck and muttered, "I'll be
back as soon as I can."

He pulled out his rifle and moved to a higher elevation
of ground and hunkered down, his eyes fixed on the dilapidated structure. This was barren land, and trees and
shrubs that would give him cover had given up the
struggle to survive. No, it would be prudent for him to
wait for the cover of darkness. Crossing this open land
would be a damned foolish thing to do.

Parnell was so weary he almost whimpered. "Elmer,
there's a house up ahead. Do you suppose we can stop
there?"

"It depends on it being unoccupied," Elmer said reflectively.

"I'm so damned tired, Elmer, I don't think I can ride
another mile."

"Are you forgetting there might be somebody after us?"

Parnell stubbornly shook his head. "I ain't forgetting a
thing. But we haven't seen signs of anybody. If they got as
far as that first shack, they probably stopped there. They'd
have to take care of the girl's body, wouldn't they?"

Elmer looked at that sullen, unhappy face. Parnell
looked on the verge of losing his mind. Anything Elmer
said to him might make Parnell run. Elmer didn't want
that. It would mean that he would be left alone, and Elmer shivered at the thought. "Maybe you're right, Odie,"
he said consolingly. "Maybe we've gone far enough for a
while. We'll look it over."

They cautiously approached the shack, and Elmer commented on its appearance. "Sure looks deserted, don't it?"
The front door sagged on one hinge, and several of the
windows were broken. An air of ruin and decay blanketed
the building.

Elmer swung down and handed his reins to Parnell. "I'll look it over." He cocked the shotgun, and holding it at his hip, walked cautiously toward the front door. He looked into the house before he entered.

Moments later, he came back out and announced, "Nobody's been here for months, but it's been occupied recently." He grinned wickedly at the way Parnell's face tightened.

"I thought you said nobody's been here," Parnell yelled.

"I'm not changing that, Odie. Tracks all over." Elmer chortled at Parnell's confusion. "Tracks made by pack rats. They're all over." He grinned at the reddening of Parnell's face. "It's a good thing the weather is clear," he went on. He enjoyed Parnell's bewilderment. "Holes all over the roof. No furniture, either, except a rusty old stove. I'm not sure it'll work."

"I don't give a goddamn," Parnell said in exasperation. "We'll have a place to stretch out, won't we?"

Elmer nodded. "That's about all. I'll go tether the horses. Any of those cans left?"

"Eight or nine."

"I'll rip a few boards off this old place. Maybe we can get a fire going in that beat-up stove."

"Right now, all I care about is stretching out," Parnell said crossly.

Elmer came back a few minutes later, carrying the gunny bag of cans. His other arm was burdened with splintered pieces of boards.

He dropped the wood before the stove. "All I could get off of the house." He laid his fire and pulled out a handful of dried grass from a pocket. "Hope this is enough to get a fire started."

Parnell watched anxiously as Elmer struck a match. The dried grass flared up immediately, and the flames licked at the wood.

"What do you know?" Elmer crowed, as the flames strengthened. "This old wreck draws." He stretched his arms in luxuriant relief. "Don't you see, Odie? This is a sign all to our good. Let those bastards tear their guts out looking for us. We've beaten them."

Parnell relaxed. He felt a pang of hunger in his belly. Maybe Elmer was right. Maybe things were turning their way.

CHAPTER 14

STEVE waited until darkness had fully settled down before he moved. Even then, he approached the shack cautiously. Motion caught the eye quicker than anything. If that dim, ghostly shack contained what he thought it did, he wasn't going to make the mistake of trying to go in and arrest the two men. No, he would wait patiently outside. He wasn't sure what he would do then. When his mind approached that point, all rational thinking went up in a fiery burst of rage.

He would pick out a point a few yards ahead of him, then crawl to it. When it was reached, he would stop and secure his position by every precaution possible. He looked and listened, and his flesh crawled at the thought that all this precaution could be wasted, that hostile eyes had already spotted him and were only waiting for him to crawl a little closer before they cut him down. Steve thought it unlikely he had been spotted, but the possibility kept his skin tight and his body sweating.

He didn't go any closer than a hundred yards. He made a half circle of the shack to see if he could spot anything that would identify the shack's occupants. He didn't see a single light anywhere in the house, and no smoke trailed from the chimney.

Three horses tethered in the back of the shack halted him. He didn't dare get any closer to identify them. A stranger approaching could pull a warning nicker from any of them. He had never seen these horses before, but the number fitted. Charley, Elmer and Parnell had taken three horses from Babcock's stable.

Steve settled back against the ground, lying flat on his back. Elmer and Parnell would come out in the morning. Steve was content to wait for that moment.

The night dragged away in its torturous passage. The last time Steve's eyes were forced open, a faint band of light showed in the eastern sky. "You've almost made it through," he told himself. Under the circumstances, that was quite an achievement. The next two hours would be the most exacting. He doubted that Elmer and Parnell would spend any more time in that shack than was necessary. No, they would be hightailing out of there as quickly as possible. This was the dangerous period for Steve, for as bone weary as he was, his mind was foggy.

He inflicted all the torture a man could inflict upon himself. He repeatedly slapped his face; he caught a cheek between thumb and forefinger and viciously twisted it. Each time his head cleared a little, chasing the fog out of his mind for a brief while.

"Ah," he said softly as the light strengthened. Elmer and Parnell were up and stirring around early, for a thin twist of smoke came out of the chimney.

What if they stay there another day? Steve thought. He groaned inaudibly. He wouldn't be able to make it by waiting. He would have to go in and get them. He didn't want to dwell on that. It would be extremely dangerous to face two deadly, determined men. They had killed before. They would not hesitate to kill again.

The waiting minutes seemed to swell into hours. Steve shifted his position constantly. The sun rose higher, and its heat added to his discomfort.

Jesus Christ, he thought furiously. Will they ever come out?

He made no sound as the door opened, but an exultant "ah" welled into his throat. Elmer Divens stepped out of the shack. He scratched himself as he looked around, then cast a glance at the sky.

Probably determining what kind of traveling weather he'll have, Steve thought. Elmer didn't know it, but his traveling days were over. Steve squirmed impatiently while waiting for Parnell to come out; Steve wanted both of them.

Elmer must be getting impatient too, for he turned his head and said something. Steve couldn't hear what he said, but he saw the opening and closing of his mouth. There must be some kind of a quarrel going on between the two, for Elmer jawed at Parnell again, and Parnell answered as heatedly.

The rifle butt was snugged against Steve's shoulder, and his eyes glinted coldly. He didn't have to fight sleep anymore, for his thoughts were clear and sharp.

The two started around the house, Elmer in the van. Steve picked him up in his sights, squinted down the barrel, and squeezed the trigger. The report sounded inordinately loud in the still morning. Steve never took his eyes off his target. If a second shot was needed, he was ready, but that shouldn't be necessary. All his hunting experience was behind that shot.

Elmer stopped as though he had run into a stone wall. He threw up his arms, half whirled, then slumped to the ground. Steve had seen enough men fall to recognize that terrible flaccidness.

He switched the rifle sights to Parnell. Parnell was frozen in shock. He didn't even know where that shot came from, and his head whipped about, trying to locate the source. He made a harried decision and plunged for the shelter of the shack. He hadn't taken more than a couple of steps when the crack of the rifle sounded again. One leg was reaching for the next stride, but the foot never touched the ground. Without the support of that leg, Parnell plunged on his face. He too lay motionless.

Steve stayed put for a moment, watching for additional movement. This was the first time he had ever shot a man from ambush, and he swallowed hard against the taste. Then all the feeble remorse was gone. Those two deserved exactly what they got.

He got up and advanced slowly toward them. He had switched the rifle to his left hand and carried his pistol in the right. A pistol shot was quicker in case another was needed.

He stood momentarily over Elmer, his face stony, his eyes bleak. Elmer was dead. The shot had taken him partially from the side, and the front of his shirt was a mass of blood.

Steve grunted unfeelingly. His eyes hadn't lost any of their old sharpness. It looked as though the bullet had coursed through Elmer's side, stopping in the heart area. If Elmer knew anything at all, it was only a vicious burst of pain that blotted out everything else. Steve hoped that in some way Sally knew about this. He moved on over to Parnell's body. Parnell lay on his back, his eyes closed. He breathed in great, laboring gasps.

Steve's second shot wasn't quite as accurate as the first, but it didn't matter. Parnell couldn't last much longer. Steve stared down at him as unfeelingly as he had looked at Elmer. Parnell's eyes slowly opened, and they were clouded with pain. He tried to say something, but his voice was so feeble Steve couldn't make out the words.

He bent over Parnell. "You trying to say something?"

"I didn't have anything to do with killing the girl. Charley raped her—" The words faded, and he wheezed with each breath.

Steve waited, his face frozen.

"She cut Charley with a butcher knife," Parnell went on. "Elmer lost his head at the sight of Charley dying. He pumped a shotgun load into her. I didn't have anything to do with it." His head fell back to the ground, and he was completely spent.

Steve's lips curled in contempt. It was just as he figured. "What did you expect? Commendation for your part in this? Your big mistake started when you threw in with the Divenses."

Parnell's eyes filled with dismay at Steve's lack of understanding. Parnell tried to say something to justify his part, and his eyes suddenly went blank and staring.

Steve bent closer to Parnell's lips. Steve could no longer hear the labored, reedy breathing. He straightened. Elmer and Parnell didn't know how lucky they were to be out of this. Their dying had been quick. It wouldn't have been if they'd been brought to trial for their crimes. He was suddenly weary of all this.

Steve walked over to the gunny bag Elmer had dropped. He picked it up and heard the clink of something metallic. It was too tinny to be money. His hand trembled as he opened the sack. There were at least a half-dozen cans in the sack. The juices started running in his mouth. He would be drooling if he didn't get those cans opened right away.

He walked to the back of the house and sat down, not wanting to eat near the two bodies. He used his hunting knife to open a can of peaches, and his hand shook so hard that he spilled some of the juice over his chin. He gulped the first few mouthfuls then slowed and cautioned himself. "Easy, or you'll wind up sick."

After finishing the first can at a slower pace, he opened the second one. The peaches had only whetted his appetite. He emptied four of the cans before the edge was gone from his hunger.

Steve leaned against the shack and patted his stomach. He could swear it was bulging. He belched and grinned. He could easily finish the last two cans, then decided against it. They were all he had to carry him back to Oklahoma City, and it was a long trip. One thing he would give a lot for right now was a cigarette, but he had finished the last quite a while back. He might not be happy, but he could live without one.

He reflected upon what to do with the two bodies in front of the shack. He knew he was going to make no attempt to bury them. He didn't need the bodies to verify his story. Dixon would take his word for it. But if Steve came in without them, something would be missing for Dixon. It wouldn't satisfy the primeval savagery in a man. Dixon needed the sight of the two dead men to quiet the lashing beast inside him.

Steve nodded and stood. He didn't like the idea. He could just as easily walk away from this spot and leave the corpses to the predators. It was going to take a toll of his strained patience, and a dozen times before he reached Oklahoma City he would be cursing Elmer and Parnell anew.

"Quit your bellyaching, Truman," he growled. "You know what you're going to do. It's not as though you don't have the transportation. You've got three horses to take back." That smile flashed again. Talking to himself was a sure sign that he'd been out here too long.

He walked back to Dixon's horse and untied it. The animal neighed, and Steve thought the sound had an accusatory note.

"I know," he said as he swung up. "It's been a rough time for both of us."

He rode back to where Elmer and Parnell lay, saddled the three horses, then fished his picket line out of a saddlebag. He hated to cut this line, but it was the only means of securing the bodies on the horses. Now would come the hard part, putting the bodies across the saddles. Steve had known few horses that didn't object violently at being burdened with an object that smelled of fresh blood.

He was right in his surmise. The horse danced nervously while he threw Elmer across the saddle. He was sweating and breathing hard when it was finally done. He used a short length of the picket line and tied Elmer's hands and feet together under the horse's belly.

"Don't you give me that much trouble," he warned the second horse.

Maybe the horse understood the warning, for the second loading went much quicker than the first. The unpleasant job was over, and Steve further mutilated his picket line by cutting it into lead ropes. He swung into the saddle and looked back at the long string of animals. It was going to be a long, slow trip back to Oklahoma City. Steve sighed at the thought filtering through his head. The sun wasn't going to do those bodies any good, either.

CHAPTER 15

IT was nearing dark when Steve finally rode into town, and lights were beginning to wink on along the street. He didn't want to arouse any undue attention as he rode toward Dixon's office, but he knew that would be impossible. A man riding at the head of a string of three horses was bound to be an attraction, particularly when they carried two corpses.

"Hey, that's Truman," Steve heard somebody yell. "Steve, what's going on?"

"Nothing," Steve snapped. He hoped his brusqueness would dissuade the curiosity seekers, but nothing could do that. The monotony in this town was so overpowering that people sought any diversion. He rode steadily ahead, ignoring the questions flung at him. Maybe his silence would be enough of a rejection to shut them up.

"Who are they, Steve? Why are you bringing them in?"

Steve was grateful that the bodies were face down. That would arouse a new wave of conjecture until people found out who the dead men were. He swung down at the hitch rack before Dixon's office. The crowd had followed him for the last three blocks, and it had swelled with every step.

Steve whirled and faced the crowd. There was no way of holding back the curious ones. "I wouldn't crowd in too close, boys," he advised. "They've been dead almost three days. They're getting pretty ripe." He turned and walked into Dixon's office, closing the door behind him. That should briefly stop them. He didn't think any of them would dare to crash that door.

Dixon didn't hear him come in. He was lost in some wracking thought, and torment rode his face. He sat just at the perimeter of the lamp's rays, and Steve was shocked at the change in his appearance. He looked twenty years older, and in just the time Steve was gone, weight had melted off of him. His collar was too big, and the skin of his neck hung as loosely as a turkey's wattles. The face was changed most of all. The flesh had been stripped away, leaving the cheekbones sharp and prominent. This man was going through pure hell.

"Did you think I'd never get back, Sam?" Steve asked softly.

Dixon started visibly, and he swung those sad eyes to Steve. "Steve," he cried and climbed awkwardly to his feet. "I was beginning to worry about you, boy," he said gruffly. "Was it rough?" He limped over to Steve and wrung his hand hard. Those anguished eyes asked a far different question, and Steve read the entreaty correctly. Did you find Sally? Is she all right?

All the way back, Steve had debated upon how to break the hideous news to Dixon. Steve had concluded there was no way of sparing him, there was no way of softening his dreadful news. Dixon would have to know, and perhaps it was best to hit him all at once and get it over with.

"I found her, Sam." The damned words insisted upon tripping over his tongue, and they came out as a squeak.

Dixon correctly read those words, or maybe it was the lack of words. All his heartbreak exploded in his eyes. He limped back to his desk and sank limply into his chair. His eyes were wide but unseeing.

The memory of those awful days returned to Steve, rearousing his fury. He didn't regret the way those two had met justice. He only wished that Charley had been alive so that he could have meted out the same treatment to him. His eyes dimmed with unshed tears, and his heart ached for the crumpled figure at the desk. It was a terrible world where three men could do to another what Charley and the other two had done to Dixon.

"She's dead, isn't she, Steve?" Dixon asked in a lifeless voice.

There was no way Steve could soften the blow. "Yes, Sam. I didn't catch up with them in time."

Dixon looked at Steve, and a new feverish fire was in his eyes. "I guess I knew it," he said falteringly, "when you didn't come back right away. The knowledge grew with each passing day." He swallowed, giving his voice time to strengthen. "They went out to my house, didn't they?"

Steve nodded numbly. How much of this should he tell Dixon? How much would be better unsaid? "They were gone when I got there," Steve said hollowly.

He had never heard such swearing before. It would rip the hide off a grizzly. Wisely, he didn't interrupt. Dixon needed all the relief he could get.

Dixon finally ran out of words, and he said brokenly, "Charley said he would get even with me. Oh that murderous bastard. I guess I didn't pay enough attention to him." He stopped and his eyes were swimming. He was close to breaking up, and only sheer will held him in line. He realized Steve was still standing, and his voice had an apologetic note. "Sit down, Steve. I want to hear all about it."

For the first time Steve saw the unfinished sandwich on a plate on Dixon's desk. No more than a couple of bites were gone. "Sam, I'm starved. I was on pretty short rations the last couple of days. If you're not going to finish that sandwich, I'd sure welcome a chance at it."

Dixon shoved the plate toward Steve. "I thought I wanted it, but I was wrong. My appetite's been poor lately. Help yourself."

Steve's hands trembled as he lifted the sandwich. The bread was soft and thick slabs of roast beef made up the filling. He could have wolfed it down in a couple of gulps, but he forced a restraint on himself. He took small nibbles, chewing each thoroughly, savoring the taste that ran through his mouth.

He talked between bites. "I tracked them into Hell's Fringe, Sam. There had been a recent rain, and those tracks weren't hard to follow." He paused to take another nibble.

Dixon leaned forward. He was emotionally strung so tight that Steve thought he would twang if something touched him.

"I caught up with them, Sam," he said soberly. "This thing had bad luck stamped all over it from the start. I was a step behind all the way." He paused, squinting across the room. How was he going to tell Dixon what had happened?

"Sally was dead," Dixon said brokenly. He raised a hand, stopping Steve's protest. "I think I knew that when you walked in here alone."

Steve sighed and slumped in his chair. Dixon's perceptiveness eliminated the worst of his task. Dixon already knew. Steve finished the sandwich while Dixon stared empty-eyed into space.

Dixon cleared his throat as Steve licked his fingers. "Was she harmed, Steve?" he asked hesitantly.

Oh God, that was the question Steve had been dreading. He could lie about it and save Dixon a lot of mental pain. "No," he said steadily. "Charley had that in mind. But Sally fought him off. You know how much spunk she had. Somehow she got hold of a butcher knife and ripped his belly open. He died hard."

Dixon's breathing came harder. "Then Elmer killed her?"

Steve eloquently spread his hands. "Yes," he said briefly. "You know how Elmer revered Charley."

Dixon's swearing started again, but all the passion was gone from the words. They were only a low, unhappy rumble of sound. The spirit that put the drive into him was all gone. "Go on," he whispered.

"I guess Elmer and Parnell buried Charley. I found the grave."

"What about Sally?" The words were brittle and tense, showing how near Dixon was to the breaking point.

"They just rode off and left her," Steve said simply. "I buried her."

Dixon smashed the desk with his fist. That was the only visible sign of protest. He seemed to shrink in size. "I wish you could have brought her back," Dixon whispered. It wasn't censure, just a forlorn wish.

"I couldn't, Sam. I had to go after Elmer and Parnell."

That put a faint spark in Dixon's eyes. "I should have

known you'd do that." A savage eagerness crept into his voice. "You caught up with them?"

Steve nodded. "I tracked them to a rundown shack. I saw the horses outside. I waited until they came out in the morning." His face tightened, and he blew out a harsh breath. "First time I ever shot a man down without giving him a chance. I shot both of them without either of them really knowing what was happening."

"Good, good," Dixon said in complete accord. Just an echo of the old toughness was in his voice. "I'd have raised hell with you if I thought you had taken chances."

Steve grinned wanly. It was good to know that Dixon didn't look at him with raised eyebrows. "I brought them back with me, Sam."

That did raise Dixon's eyebrows. "Why?" he demanded. "I'd have left them out there for the buzzards."

"I don't know," Steve said helplessly. "I thought it might give you some kind of satisfaction if you saw them."

Dixon saw how distressed Steve was, for Dixon said, "You did right. I'd like to look at the two bastards who had a hand in killing my daughter." He stood and reached for his hat. "I'd enjoy seeing that carrion."

Steve followed Dixon outdoors. The crowd had grown noticeably since Steve entered the marshal's office. Steve heard the excited hum of their talk, though at this distance he couldn't make out any words.

"Clear the way," Dixon barked. He limped straight ahead, and people parted to make passage.

"Hey, Sam," a man called, "your deputy did good. He brought in two of the Divens gang. Too bad he didn't get Charley, too."

They had looked at the faces of the two bodies, Steve thought. Their stomachs must be strong to get close enough to identify Elmer and Parnell.

"Charley's buried," Dixon announced in a flat voice. His face didn't lose that hard, frozen look at the cheers that rose. The Divens gang had never been liked. Their killing spree before they left Oklahoma City had only intensified the dislike. Steve could just imagine what that reaction would be if they knew Sally was included in that spree. He didn't see any use saying anything about her. Dixon would have dozens of questions hammered at him, and he was suffering enough as it was.

"I got Charley first," Steve said soberly. "I had to go farther to get those two." He jerked his head at the burdened horses.

A short, stocky man pushed his way through the crowd. He had a positive, authoritative manner that swept all opposition before it. He planted himself before Steve. "I'm Lowell Graves, correspondent for the Kansas City *Star*."

Steve didn't respond, though he wondered why the Kansas City *Star* would send a reporter all this distance. He waited for Graves to go on.

"My editor sent me down here," Graves explained. "He wanted to know how the newly opened territory is doing." He glanced at the two dangling bodies, and he displayed dazzling teeth in a wide smile. "Looks as though the stories we've heard about life being wild down here wasn't far wrong, was it?"

"It's not as wild as it used to be," Dixon said drily.

For a moment, Graves looked confused as to Dixon's meaning, then he glanced at the two bodies again. He figured out Dixon's meaning and said smoothly, "I guess it isn't. Did those two cause you a lot of grief?"

Oh Lord, Steve mourned. The man's choice of words couldn't be worse. "Enough," he said through clenched teeth. "The Divens gang killed three men while breaking out of jail. And they were already up on a murder charge."

Graves had a notebook, and he was busy jotting down fragments of Steve's words. "Which one of you got these two?"

"My deputy, Steve Truman," Dixon interrupted. "And there were three of them. I guess you didn't hear what Steve said just a moment ago."

Graves shook his head. "I just came up. Were there more of them?"

"Charley Divens was the leader," Dixon said. "Steve got him, too. He didn't bring him in."

Graves' eyes widened. "That could have been a dangerous job, Mr.——" He paused, waiting for Dixon to mention his name.

"Sam Dixon," Dixon grunted. "United States marshal. I had a gimpy leg and thought Steve would do a better job. I was right."

Graves wrote rapidly, turning over a page. "The citizens

of this town should be grateful to your deputy for ridding the community of such dangerous men."

"They are. Didn't you hear them yelling for Steve?" He started to untie his horse, and Graves hurried after him.

"Was there a reward for these men, Marshal?"

Dixon shook his head in the negative.

"I think there should have been," Graves stated.

"Yes," Dixon agreed and finished untying his horse.

"Just a moment more," Graves begged. "I want to be sure I have the names straight." He hesitated, his pencil poised.

"I'm Sam Dixon. My deputy is Steve Truman."

"And the names of the dead men," Graves said.

"Elmer Divens and Odie Parnell. There were three of them when they started. Charley, brother of Elmer, led the gang."

Graves finished writing and asked, "Wouldn't you like to have a copy of the paper when the story comes out?"

Dixon peered at Steve, and Steve shook his head. He wasn't that anxious to see his name in a paper. The sooner he forgot all about this, the better off he would be.

Dixon shrugged. "Doesn't make much difference to either of us." He started limping off again, leading the string of horses. This time, Graves let him go.

Steve caught up with him. "He asked a hell of a lot of questions," he complained.

"That's his business." Dixon stared straight ahead.

Steve was concerned about the thoughts running through Dixon's mind. "Where are we going now, Sam?"

"To take the bodies to Andrews." Dixon's face twisted. "Though I don't mind telling you, if it was my decision, I'd dump this carrion in the street and let the dogs have them." He scowled at Steve. "If that shocks you, I don't give a damn."

"Who's blaming you?" Steve asked mildly. "I shot these men in the back. After Andrews, where then?"

"I'm telling Andrews my office isn't paying for their burial. I don't care what he does with them."

Steve grimaced. "You made that clear. I asked where do we go after Andrews?"

Dixon stared straight ahead again. He had retreated into his own private world once more. But he heard Steve's question, for he answered, "Back to Babcock's livery stable. I don't know who's running it now, but whoever it is can get word to the former owners that we have their horses. That should about wrap up everything."

Steve glanced covertly at the misery-ridden face. This would never be wrapped up for either of them.

CHAPTER 16

Two weeks had passed since Steve returned to Oklahoma City. Those two weeks had made a drastic change in Dixon. He was silent to the point of moroseness, and Steve didn't try to push him. Two weeks weren't long enough to wipe out the loss of Sally.

Dixon asked the same question every morning when he came in. "That Kansas City paper come in yet?"

It was one of Steve's minor chores to stop by the post office to pick up the mail. Each morning he had answered Dixon's question with a negative shake of his head. Yesterday, curiosity had overcome him, and he asked, "Sam, why so much interest in that paper? I thought you didn't give a damn one way or the other."

Dixon wouldn't meet his eyes. "A man can change his mind, can't he?" he asked crossly.

Steve didn't push the subject further. That was an indication of how Dixon's mood had changed. Formerly, he was an easygoing man with time to listen to everybody. Now he was withdrawn and sullen. In two weeks' time, Dixon had shot two men, killing one and seriously wounding the other. Both of them were lawbreakers, but it was so unlike Dixon that the whole town buzzed about the incidents. Steve had done a lot of wondering himself. Before, Dixon resorted to a gun only when he was driven to it. On these occasions he hadn't been driven. In fact, the few witnesses who saw the incidents said that Dixon had pushed the confrontation, egging his opponents on until they foolishly tried to outdraw him.

Dixon was still glaring at him, and Steve said easily, "He can change his mind as often as he wants to, Sam."

"Don't you forget it," Dixon growled. He jammed his hat on his head and limped out of the office.

Steve was unhappy as he looked after him. Steve was almost reaching the point where he didn't want to be a lawman anymore. Working at this job was no longer interesting, particularly since Dixon had changed. Dixon didn't talk anymore; he snapped. Already, two deputies had quit their jobs. Steve could appreciate their feeling. Much more of this, and he'd be ready to take the same road. He didn't blame Dixon; Steve sympathized with him in every way. But it didn't make living around him any easier.

It was time to make another round of the town. Maybe he should stop in the post office to see if any mail had come in. It was damned curious how interested Dixon had become in the mail.

He walked into the post office and asked the postmaster, "Any mail, Jeb?"

"What's happened to make you people so interested in the mail?" Jenkins growled as he got up out of his chair. "Getting so a man can't rest his bones without somebody plaguing him." He moved heavily to the bank of pigeon-holes.

Steve grinned. "A man's got to keep up with what's going on."

Jenkins came back with a folded-up newspaper in his hand. "That's all there is. Don't seem worthwhile to make a trip down here just for this." He handed the newspaper to Steve.

Steve unfolded it. A bold headline seemed to jump off the page: "BRAVE LAWMAN HOLDS DOWN CRIME IN OKLAHOMA CITY."

Steve's face burned as he read on. Graves had done a lurid job in reporting this new crushing of lawlessness. He made it sound as though Steve was the only man in the world fighting crime. He refolded the paper and thrust it in his pocket. Damn, he didn't want anybody seeing him read this.

He walked back to the office, and Dixon was seated at his desk. Steve tossed the paper before him. "Here's that newspaper you were so interested in," he said sourly. He pretended disinterest as Dixon unfolded the paper and scanned it, but Steve kept glancing at him.

Dixon read snatches of the story aloud. " 'Deputy smashes the Divens gang. It took raw courage to go up against those three desperadoes.' "

"Oh, cut it out," Steve said peevishly. "I shot two of them in the back. I'm not exactly proud of that. I didn't kill Charley and you know it."

For the first time in days, Dixon grinned at him. "But Graves didn't know that. He put down what you told him. If you left something out, it wasn't his fault." He chortled as he read on. "He got our names right. 'Under the able direction of Marshal Dixon, Deputy Steve Truman did a necessary job. Without this kind of man all law would break down completely in the territory. I saw the bodies of Elmer Divens and Odie Parnell, brought in by the above-named deputy. Deputy Truman stated he buried Charley Divens earlier. Singlehandedly, he accounted for a wicked, lawless gang.' " Dixon glanced at Steve. "Doesn't that make you feel important?"

"Oh hell," Steve said in disgust. "With that news account and a nickel, I can buy a cup of coffee anyplace in town."

Dixon resumed his reading. " 'The good people of Oklahoma Territory can be grateful that they have such men protecting them.' " He laid the paper down. "Now what do you think?"

"A lot of crap," Steve growled. "I didn't do anything to get special credit for. I only did my job."

"Maybe you've got it all wrong," Dixon said, shaking his head. "Sure, Graves blew it up a little. But in the main he told what happened."

"I never saw you so damned interested in publicity," Steve growled. "All of a sudden, you seem to be hungering for it. That damned newspaper story won't change anything for either of us."

"Maybe you're wrong again." Dixon's complacency was as close as Steve had seen him come to good humor in the days since he had come back. "The day after you returned, I sent a long wire to the Secretary of the Interior John W. Noble. It cost me a pretty penny but if it turns out like I hope it will, it's worth it. I told him all about you tracking down the Divens gang and bringing back two of them. I also mentioned you'd buried Charley Divens, wiping out the whole gang. I told him about breaking jail while waiting for a jury trial for murder. Three more lives lost in that jailbreak. I suggested that you should be rewarded. Noble is interested in Oklahoma affairs. He has influence in Congress. The way Congress has been throwing money around, a piddling matter of reward money shouldn't stick in their craws."

"Oh my God," Steve moaned. "Where did you get such a fool idea?"

"Graves put it in my mind when he said you should be rewarded. I pointed out to Noble that you had already saved the government a big sum of money. The Divens gang won't have to be tried."

Steve kept shaking his head. "That makes me look like a bloodsucker. You didn't hear from him, did you?"

"You're wrong on every count," Dixon said disparagingly. "I heard from him the following day. He agreed with every point I made, but there was one big obstacle blocking him from going before Congress to ask for the reward: proof. All he had was my say-so. He needed more."

"That's all you'll hear of it," Steve said in triumph.

"Wrong once more, Steve." Dixon lifted the copy of the Kansas City *Star*. "That reporter saw those bodies and put it down in black and white. Here's Noble's proof."

"Christ," Steve said. "So that's why you were so interested in that copy getting here."

"You're getting brighter," Dixon said.

"How much did you ask for?" Steve asked curiously.

"Twenty-five hundred dollars," Dixon replied calmly. "Don't give me an argument about it being too much. If the Divens gang had stayed alive, how many more lives do you think they would have taken? A half dozen, a dozen? I don't give a damn, if it was only one. Twenty-five hundred is still a cheap price for a human life."

Steve whistled soundlessly. Twenty-five hundred dollars! That was more money than he had ever dreamed of. "Nothing will happen," he said, and he couldn't quite make his voice steady.

"It'll take some time," Dixon replied with that maddening assurance. "Just wait. You'll see."

Steve could feel the heat creeping up under his collar. "Did I ask you to do this for me?" he demanded.

Dixon's deepening color was in response to the bite in

Steve's words. "Steve, it was the only thing I could do to make some kind of repayment for—" He paused and gestured helplessly.

"Say it plainer," Steve snapped.

For a moment, Dixon's lips were a tight, pinched line. "For what you did for Sally. If it hadn't been for you, they could've gotten clean away."

"Oh damn it," Steve said hotly. "Did you think money was my reason?"

"I know it wasn't," Dixon replied gravely. "But this was the only thing I could see to do."

Steve stood. He better get out of here before he lost his temper. "I just wish you hadn't thought of anything," he said flatly.

CHAPTER 17

Linus Divens limped out to the mailbox. He peered into it and cussed. He must be too early; the box was empty. He looked back at the rundown house, a mile outside of Harrison, Arkansas. He shook his head. The house was getting in a terrible shape. It was badly in need of painting, and the roof needed repairs. Two windows needed replacing, and there were a dozen other things that needed fixing. He guessed all the repairing would have to wait until Charley and Elmer sent him more money. The Lord knew that he was barely making enough to live on off these few hardscrabble acres. All the work in the world couldn't produce more from this miserable land. That was the main reason that ran Charley and Elmer off.

Linus knew they were talking about it a good six months before they left. And that Odie Parnell was always in on the conversations that were quickly broken off when Linus appeared. But he knew they were planning something. He had heard several disjointed remarks such as, "It don't do no good to work your ass off on this rock pile. There's gotta be a better way to make a living."

Linus wasn't surprised when his two boys approached him. Charley announced, "Pa, we're leaving."

Linus didn't let surprise touch his face. "Odie going with you?"

That started Charley. "How'd you know that?"

Linus grunted and scratched himself. "Saw you three talking together often enough."

Linus' eyes were empty as he remembered. Things had gotten worse with Charley and Elmer not being around to share the work. Linus remembered the last thing he had said, trying to hold them home: "Think of what you'll be giving up. You got a home here."

Charley had laughed coarsely. "You don't call this a home, do you, Pa?"

"Have you got better?" Linus asked indignantly.

"We'll find something better," Charley said cockily. "Ain't that right, Elmer?"

"Sure as hell is, Charley," Elmer replied, grinning broadly.

Linus sighed moodily as he recalled that parting. He hadn't gotten much out of them. Charley had vaguely said something about going to Oklahoma.

"That's nothing but a wilderness," Linus had objected. He hadn't been able to dissuade them. They had ridden off on those two tired old horses. Linus hadn't tried to stop them. Charley was mean-tempered: He would have taken them anyway.

Linus considered returning to the house, but that would only mean a return trip to the mailbox, and even that short distance took a tremendous effort with his gimpy leg. It never had been right after that mule's kick had broken it.

Linus guessed things had started going downhill after Maude died. Now all he had left at home was Cleatis, his sixteen-year-old son. Cleatis had wanted to go with his brothers, but Charley had scoffed at him. "What would we do with a snot-nosed kid tagging us everywhere we went?"

The flush in Cleatis' face showed how much that hurt him, but that was Charley's way. He didn't care who he trod on. He treated Elmer better; maybe that was why Elmer adored him.

Linus shifted his weight. Standing there was beginning

to make his gimpy leg hurt. Damned if he was going to stand out here much longer waiting for some damned mailman.

Nothing had happened the first four months after Charley and Elmer left. How he remembered his joy at receiving a letter from Charley. "Dear Pa," he read. "Things are going just swell. Elmer and I are doing fine. Enclosed is two hundred dollars. Will send you more as things improve."

Linus couldn't remember a time when he held this much money in his hand. He wondered uneasily what Charley and Elmer were doing. It was probably something illegal, but he knew better than to ask. He couldn't blame his boys for being covetous when so many people around them were raking in money with both hands. Besides, he didn't know where Charley and Elmer were. The postmark was smudged, and he couldn't make out the town of its origin.

Linus had done a lot of good with that money. Not as many repairs as he set out to do, but he and Cleatis had made a few. Most of the money went for good food and good booze. Linus had never lived so high in his life.

Letters kept dribbling in, but never with huge amounts of money. Several times there had been fifty dollars and, once, a hundred. Linus didn't care what Elmer and Charley were doing. Whatever it was, he wished them success.

He peered down the road, seeing indistinct motion. By God, he believed that old Tote Thomas was finally coming. Linus shifted his weight to his one good leg, beginning to breathe hard. It had been several months since he had heard from his boys. It could happen any day now. His boys wouldn't let him down.

"Howdy, Linus," Thomas said as he pulled up the rack of bones that drew the dilapidated buggy.

"Took you long enough," Linus said ungraciously.

Thomas was well up in his sixties, and he had learned to let complaints roll off his back. "Had a hell of a route," he said in explanation. "Seemed like everybody got letters today."

Linus' eyes gleamed. If the mail was that good, this could be the day when he heard from Charley and Elmer.

Thomas handed him a folded newspaper.

"This all?" Linus asked, disappointment plain on his face.

"It's all I give you, ain't it?" Thomas said with asperity. "If there was more, I'd have handed it to you."

"Expecting a letter from the boys," Linus mumbled. "Overdue now."

"You say the same thing every time I come by here. You get on their backs for not writing. Not mine." Thomas slapped the reins on the tired rump of the horse. "Come on, Dolly. We got quite a way to go before this day's over."

Linus stared disappointedly after him. He wondered if there had been a letter for him. It was entirely possible. Somebody in the post office had found out that he received occasional sums of money. Maybe old Thomas could be the guilty one. Linus' shoulders slumped as he turned toward the house. How in the hell was he going to prove that the post office was a nest of thieves? He didn't have the slightest idea of whom to turn to. The sheriff wouldn't listen to him.

He pulled off the twine binding the newspaper and started unrolling it. He didn't know why he had subscribed to this fool Kansas City paper. He didn't give a damn what happened in Kansas City. He was going to stop his subscription the first chance he had.

A bold headline leaped out at him, and his eyes bulged. Something about a brave lawman cutting down three criminals.

He read on, his throat going tight. Charley and Elmer and Odie made three. It couldn't be. He was wheezing hard as he mumbled the names aloud. Deputy Steve Truman had brought in the bodies of Elmer and Odie. Worse, he had buried Charley earlier. Marshal Dixon said the Divens gang was responsible for four known murders, maybe more that hadn't been discovered. Linus' eyes swam, and he couldn't get his breath. That damned marshal was a liar. Linus couldn't be sure about Odie, but he knew his two boys weren't murderers.

He lumbered up to the porch, hurrying as fast as he could. He started bawling at the top of his lungs as he stepped onto the porch. "Cleatis," he roared, "get out here." He feverishly paced the porch. Where was that damned boy? "Cleatis," he yelled. He put all his lung power into it.

Cleatis finally shuffled out onto the porch. He was six-teen years old, but in physical size far beyond his years. Unfortunately, although he had matured physically, his smooth, dull face said he hadn't progressed nearly as far mentally. "You sure raising a lot of hell, Pa," he said querulously. "Something eating on you?"

"I yelled my head off for you. What were you doing?"

"Just sitting in the kitchen, Pa. Not doing much of any-thing."

"You never are," Linus complained. His loss was a physical ache. Two of his boys were gone. Why couldn't it have been this one instead of Charley and Elmer?

Cleatis' face didn't change under Linus' tirade. It looked the same as usual: dull and heavy. "You want something in particular, Pa?"

Linus thrust the paper at him. "Read this." A forefinger indicated the story he meant.

Cleatis sighed. "You know I don't read so well, Pa." He saw Linus' face working and sighed. "I'll try, Pa. If I have trouble with some of the words, don't you be blaming me." He stumbled through the account, tripping over one word after another.

Linus looked at his son's dull eyes. None of this was making any sense to him.

Cleatis' face suddenly lit up as he recognized a few familiar words. "Hey, here's Charley's and Elmer's names. Is this all about them?"

"About them," Linus said grimly. "They're dead."

Cleatis stared at him open-mouthed, and his lips trembled. "Dead? How could that be?"

Linus snatched the paper from his hands. "Didn't you read those other names? Marshal Dixon and Deputy Steve Truman?"

Cleatis shook his head. "Guess I just passed them over."

"They're the ones responsible for your brothers' deaths. Marshal Dixon sent that Deputy Truman to go out and shoot them down."

Cleatis stared at him, his eyes wide and uncomprehend-ing. "Why would he want to do that?"

"You remember all that money Charley and Elmer sent us?"

Unconsciously, Cleatis licked his mouth. Yes, he remembered those times well. They had eaten good. "Are they going to send us some more, Pa?"

"Oh, goddamn it," Linus raged. "Don't you understand anything? They're dead. That marshal and deputy killed them, for no reason at all." His eyes narrowed. He had to have a reason that would inflame Cleatis. "Unless they were jealous of Charley and Elmer. Their success was more than little men could stand."

Cleatis' soft, doughy mouth rounded into a soundless O. "Why, that ain't right," he complained.

"It sure ain't, son. Now there won't be any more letters with money in them."

Cleatis' heavy hands closed and opened spasmodically. "I wish I could see those two," he said petulantly.

A soft sigh escaped Linus' lips. He had Cleatis thinking right. "Maybe you can, son. They're in Oklahoma City, in that new land just opened."

The dullness remained in Cleatis' eyes. Linus had read to him all about the opening of Oklahoma Territory, but Cleatis had forgotten. Going back through it all would be hopeless.

"Oklahoma City isn't too far from here, Cleatis. It's over in that direction." Linus stabbed a finger toward the west. "You could go there and show the marshal and deputy they've done wrong."

Cleatis licked his lips. "How would I do that?"

"Damn it," Linus said hotly. "Those two shot down your brothers. Are you just going to forget how good those brothers were to you? Charley taught you how to shoot a rifle. Hell, he even gave you his old rifle."

Cleatis' face brightened. "He sure did. I got pretty good with it, didn't I, Pa?"

Linus nodded. "All of that doesn't mean anything if you don't do something about that marshal and deputy."

Cleatis' eyes went round. He thought he was beginning to understand what his Pa was driving at. "Do you want me to go to Oklahoma City and shoot them?" His voice was an awed whisper.

"They got it coming, ain't they?" Linus said fiercely. "For no reason at all, they just shoot down Charley and Elmer." He tried to look grief-stricken. "Just forget it. If your brothers don't mean any more than this to you—" He let the sentence fade into a doleful sigh.

"Pa," Cleatis cried in immediate agony, "I didn't say that. I just don't know how to get there, or how I'm going to do it. I ain't got a dime in my pockets."

Linus reached into his pocket and pulled out a five-dollar bill. "Here, Cleatis. You take this. It'll carry you to Oklahoma City by stretching it out. You go to Harrison and ask directions to Oklahoma City. Somebody will know. After they tell you, you just set out. You're bound to get occasional rides. Wagons will pass along and give you a lift. Even if they don't, it ain't impossible to walk to Oklahoma City. It won't take long. Just keep thinking about getting even with the two men responsible for your brothers' deaths."

It was rare that Cleatis' eyes fired, but they were firing now. "I'll do it, Pa," he cried. A thought struck him, and he yelped in distress. "Pa, how am I going to know them when I see them?"

"That's easy," Linus scoffed. "The marshal and his deputy are bound to be well known in Oklahoma City. Just ask somebody to point them out to you. Got that straight?"

Cleatis nodded dubiously. "I think so, Pa."

"Good. Go into the house and put on your best clothes." He glanced at Cleatis' bare feet. "And your boots too. You ain't going to get very far walking barefoot." Cleatis' face clouded, and Linus demanded, "Now what's wrong?"

"All I've got is the boots you bought me two years ago."

"Yes, and you haven't worn them long enough to fairly break them in."

"I've gotten bigger. They hurt my feet."

"When you come to a stream you can take off your boots and soak your feet. That'll ease them, won't it?"

Cleatis' face cleared. His pa knew the answer to anything. "One other thing, Pa. When I get to Oklahoma City, shall I tell people who I am?"

"Jesus Christ, no," Linus exploded. "You don't tell nobody."

"Pa, I only got a dozen shells," Cleatis said worriedly.

"You won't need more than two," Linus pointed out, his face severe. "If you run out, you can buy some more."

Cleatis brightened. "Say, that's right. So long, Pa."

Cleatis went down the steps, looking back several times.

Linus sat on the porch, watching Cleatis go down the lane to the road. Linus was sending his last son. It was going to be powerful lonesome around here, but he wouldn't be able to rest until he knew that Marshal Dixon and Deputy Truman were taken care of.

Linus thumbed a welling tear from his eyes. This was a rough old life. A man was constantly called upon to make sacrifices.

CHAPTER 18

It had been a little over a month since Dixon and Steve had discussed the possibility of a reward for Steve. They had come perilously close to heated words, and the subject hadn't come up again. Steve was just as happy that it hadn't. That reward would never happen, and that's the way Steve wanted it. Each day he came to the office half fearful that Dixon would bring the subject up again, but he hadn't.

Steve finished his round of the town and came in, nodding to Dixon. Things had gotten so bad that they rarely spoke to each other unless it was on official business. There just wasn't anything to talk about anymore, Steve thought miserably.

"Quiet?" Dixon asked curtly.

Steve nodded without speaking.

Dixon reached into a desk drawer, pulled out a folded newspaper and tossed it to Steve.

"What's this for, Sam?"

"Remember you saying there would never be a reward? Read it and find out how wrong you are. Graves attached a note to the paper. He wrote, 'Thought you might be interested in this.' Go on. Read it."

Steve unwillingly opened the paper. He was sorry he had ever talked to Graves. The headline stated that Congress met to discuss rewarding the deputy who had wiped out the Divens gang. The House unanimously voted to see that Steve Truman was rewarded for his heroic efforts. The reward was to be twenty-five hundred dollars, as suggested by Secretary Noble. Secretary Noble said the Senate had to pass on the reward, but he was certain that was only a formality. He believed the reward would be in Truman's hands in two weeks or less. Steve laid down the paper and stared blankly at the ceiling. He was too stunned to think straight.

"You're not thinking of refusing it, Steve?" Dixon said, appalled. "It's your money. Congress voted it for you."

Steve's shoulders sagged. Once Dixon had an idea lodged in his mind, it had to be blasted out. Steve's face brightened as an idea occurred to him. "I'll tell you what we'll do, Sam. We'll split the money right down the middle."

Dixon looked at him with such repugnance that Steve was shocked. "Hell, no," he shouted. "Taking money because my little girl died, why, that'd be blood money."

Steve couldn't see where this argument was going to end any better than the first. "Then just send it back to Congress," he said, his jaw set stubbornly.

"You can't do that," Dixon said frantically.

"Why can't I?"

Dixon searched helplessly for an explanation. "Because it's already issued. I think there's a law against taking it back. It messes up their books."

Steve looked cynically at him. Dixon was trying to mix him up with these phony excuses. He got to his feet. "You do what you want with it. I told you I don't want it." He strode out of the office, his hat set firmly on his head.

Another two weeks passed. Neither Steve nor Dixon spoke of the money again. Jeb Jenkins came in one morning, and he carried an official-looking envelope in his hand.

"Thought I'd drop by and bring you this." Curiosity dripped from Jenkins like sweat on a hot day.

"Since when did you start delivering mail?" Dixon growled. "Up to now, you'd let a letter stay in your post office for weeks without doing anything about it."

Jenkins colored. "This is government business. I thought it needed to be rushed."

"Who's it for?" Dixon snapped.

Jenkins had to raise the envelope close to his old eyes to make out the addressee. "It's for Steve."

"Then hand it to him," Dixon said impatiently.

Jenkins handed over the letter. He shifted his weight, and the curiosity was now chewing big chunks out of him. "Ain't you going to open it?" he asked disappointedly.

Steve grinned tauntingly. "Not now, Jeb. I got other things to do."

Jenkins helplessly wrung his hands, glancing imploringly at Dixon.

Dixon had no sympathy for him. "Don't you have something to do at the post office? Don't seem like it the way you're standing around."

"It's probably that reward money," Dixon remarked after Jenkins had left. Steve pulled a knife out of a pocket, opened a blade, and split the envelope open. The letter inside was from Secretary Noble. It was filled with laudatory words, and Steve read them hurriedly. His eyes riveted on the official-looking check issued by the United States Treasury. "I'll be goddamned," he said in a dazed voice. The check was made out for twenty-five hundred dollars. That was the most impressive figure Steve had ever looked at. Wordless, he handed the letter and check to Dixon.

Dixon read the letter. " 'bout time this office got some recognition," he grunted. "Lord, the Secretary praises you high enough. He makes it sound like you're cleaning up Oklahoma singlehanded."

Steve flushed. "I told you I didn't want the money. I didn't start all this."

"But doesn't that letter make you feel good? Do what you want with the check. You can try to send it back, or cash it and spend it."

Steve's indignation hadn't abated. "What would I spend that much money on?"

Dixon grinned twistedly. "It's not hard to spend money in this town. Spend it on women or gamble it away. Either can take it away quick enough." His face sobered. "My advice is to bank it. At least, it'll give you time to think it over." He handed the letter and check back to Steve. "I'm proud of you, Steve."

Steve glared at the check. He still felt the same way about this money. He took a stride toward the door, then paused. "Maybe I'll bank it until I think it over. It's not smart to walk around this town with a pocketful of money."

"Good," Dixon approved. "Now you're starting to use your head."

"Pure crap," Steve said in disgust and walked out.

CHAPTER 19

CLEATIS plodded on steadily toward the town he saw on the horizon. That ought to be Oklahoma City. Lord, it had taken him long enough to reach it. Linus hadn't been right about all those rides being offered him. In all this distance, he had been offered only two, and they had been only for short distances.

Cleatis looked down at his dusty boots. At least they didn't hurt anymore. The walking had finally broken them in. He was pretty proud of himself for the way he accomplished this trip. He hadn't spent his money on food or lodging, but slept every night under the stars. He grimaced at the thought of the three rainy nights. That hadn't been too comfortable, but he accepted the discomforts stoically. He hadn't spent any money on food, either, but had subsisted mostly on fruit, gathered along the road, and small game.

He felt a swelling of pride as he walked along. He had come all this way, and still hadn't broken the five-dollar bill. He knew that at times Linus worried about him getting along. This time, Linus was wrong.

Cleatis stopped on the outskirts of Oklahoma City. At least, he hoped it was. He had come all this distance without seeing a map. He couldn't have read it anyway. Every so often, he stopped somebody and asked directions. Those fingers always pointed west. How could he have gone wrong?

The deeper he walked into town, the more confused he became. It was so big and noisy. He had never seen a town anywhere like this one. Harrison was quiet and sub-

dued by comparison. People went about their business
there, never raising a fuss. Here they shouted and cursed
at the top of their voices. One minute, they'd be laughing
loudly together; the next they were fighting.

Cleatis saw two men knocked down. They struggled for
a while on the ground. One of them trying to get back on
his feet was cut. Cleatis shivered at the sight of the flowing
blood. He had never used a knife, or seen one used this
way. The wounded man, holding his belly together, staggered a few paces, then fell dead.

Cleatis had the answer as to why this town was so wild.
There was no proper law. Harrison had old Cal Duncan as
their sheriff. He had been in the office longer than Cleatis
could remember, and he ran Harrison with a firm hand. If
something like this had happened there, Duncan would
have a hand clamped on the back of the criminal's neck
before he got a dozen steps away.

Nobody seemed to pay any attention to this incident.
The man wielding the knife stood and walked by the dead
man without a second glance. Passersby walked by the
body without attempting to offer any help.

The law here had to be weak and ineffective when
something like this was allowed to happen. Cleatis stopped
short as a thought struck him. That was why Charley and
Elmer were dead. The law hadn't made any effort to protect his brothers.

He was ambling by a livery stable when a portly man,
sitting in the shade of the runway, called to him. "Hey
you. Hold up a moment."

Cleatis slowly turned, his face wary. A city and its ways
were confusing.

"You come from the country?" the man asked. At
Cleatis' nod he got up. "You look big enough to do a decent day's work. Want to go to work for me? I'll pay you
seventy-five cents a day. If you work real good, I might
raise it later."

Cleatis' excitement made his breathing faster. "What
would I do?"

"Mainly clean out the stalls. As other things come in
mind I'll tell you."

Cleatis' eyes glowed. That was a magnificent salary.
Why, he could eat on that much money. The only trouble
would be that he had no place to sleep without paying for
it. He clung to that five-dollar bill with a sort of desperate

intensity. Not spending it was proof to Linus that he was old enough to handle money.

The portly man scowled at Cleatis' hesitation. "What's wrong now?" At Cleatis' gulp he said impatiently, "You can tell Holt Jorman. When he makes a commitment, he keeps it. Tell me what you see wrong with the job."

"I need a place to sleep."

Jorman laughed. "I can take care of that. You can sleep on a cot in the tackroom."

Cleatis' eyes blazed with joy. Everything had fallen into place for him. He had a job paying enough money to live on and a place to sleep. Linus would be proud of him.

"Do we have a deal?" Jorman demanded.

Cleatis took an unsteady breath. "We sure do. When do I start?"

"How about right now? Come on, I'll show you." Jorman stopped at the first stall. It had been many a day since it had been cleaned. He picked up a pitchfork, and before he handed it to Cleatis, said, "I'd like to know who I'm hiring."

"Cleatis—" He swallowed hard, then said, "Cleatis Dudley."

Jorman caught that brief hesitation. That wasn't his real name. Probably on the run from something. Jorman didn't give a damn what Cleatis had done as long as he was a good worker. He handed over the pitchfork and pointed out a wheelbarrow. "There's a dozen stalls to clean," he warned.

Cleatis trundled the wheelbarrow into position, then bent to his work. He was a lucky man. Handling manure wasn't that much work.

Jorman watched Cleatis work for a few minutes. This country boy was a bear for work. He started at a fast pace and never slackened. He pushed the filled wheelbarrow out and dumped it on a small manure pile. He came back and his breathing wasn't even labored.

"You did that pretty fast," Jorman commented. "I'd like to see you stay on here."

Cleatis' eyes rounded. "What would stop me from staying?"

"Only two things I can think of: booze and women. Both of them can wreck a man."

Cleatis shook his head. "I don't drink, and I'm afraid of women." He shook his head, dismissing everything Jorman mentioned. Cleatis was whistling when he returned to work.

Jorman watched him for a few moments more, then moved back to his chair. He sat down, completely satisfied. He saw enough in the small time he watched Cleatis to know he had hired himself a damn good worker. Jorman's eyes slowly closed, and he floated in contentment. The last four stablehands he hired hadn't been worth a damn. But that was about the only kind of help available. They were shiftless, lazy drifters who didn't want to work an honest hour for honest pay. It was like he'd always said: Go to the country when you want a good worker.

CHAPTER 20

FOR three days after Dixon handed over the check, Steve walked around with it in his pocket. But that made him nervous. Even though it was a check and would be hard for anybody but him to cash, it was dangerous walking around Oklahoma City with that much money.

"Oh what the hell," he growled and wheeled to retrace his steps to the bank he had passed just a moment ago.

He couldn't remember when he had last been in a bank. On his salary there had been no need to go to one. The sign over the door read, "First National Bank of Oklahoma City." It was more imposing than the rest of the building, which had been thrown up hastily, and the poor workmanship showed. The boards were from pine trees near town. They were green and already beginning to twist and draw apart under the hot Oklahoma sun. Steve could see cracks in the sideboards, some of them as wide as his little finger.

It was a flimsy-looking building, and he worried about it. Maybe this wasn't a safe place for his money. Then he saw the safe at the rear of the room. It was a chunky, solid piece of iron, half as tall as a man. Steve would bet that a stout wagon couldn't haul that safe away. He could forget his concern about security.

It was the first time he had been inside, and he looked around curiously. It had a raw, new look, and was in need of paint. But it was far better than the tents of Oklahoma City. Maybe the people running this bank were too busy to tend to decorating this building. It did have a bustling air of prosperity. A fairly long line of customers was standing before the grillwork surrounding a small cage where a lone man worked.

Steve worked his way up the line until he stood before the teller. "Mungo North," he exclaimed, thoroughly surprised.

"Hello, Steve," North greeted him. North was thin almost to the point of scrawniness. His shoulders were stooped, and he had the pallor of an indoor man.

Steve knew him to speak to. They had shared a few meals together and talked over a drink now and then. But in all that exchange of conversation, Steve hadn't learned what North's business was. "I didn't know you worked in the bank," Steve said, feeling a little foolish.

"You never asked me," North replied, smiling. "And you've never been in here before." North was a likable man, mild of manner and gentle in appearance. It was too bad Oklahoma City's population didn't contain a greater percentage of people like him. "What can I do for you, Steve?"

"I thought I'd open an account, Mungo."

"Smart," North approved. "A man saves a few dollars here and a few dollars there, and before he knows it, he's got a chunk of money on his hands."

"Been considering that," Steve said solemnly. He pulled the folded check from his shirt pocket and straightened it out before North. He couldn't help but chuckle at the way North's eyes bugged. "You choking on something, Mungo?" he asked gently.

"My God," North gasped. "The size of this check. I've got to treat you with more respect. You're a man of wealth." Though he hadn't asked a question, his eyes were curious.

"The government figured it owed me this money," Steve explained and let it go at that.

North didn't pry. He entered the amount in a passbook

and handed it over. "Steve, a bit of advice. I'm not trying to step on your toes." He waited anxiously for Steve's reaction.

"Go ahead, Mungo."

"Leaving this money in the bank won't do you any good. You ought to invest it in a business of some kind. It'd make you a better return on your money. Just laying here in the bank won't make you a dime."

"What am I going to do about my job?" Steve asked. "I can't hold my job and run a business, too. Besides, I wouldn't know what business to go into."

"There's dozens of opportunities opening up every day, Steve. If a man keeps his eyes open, he's bound to pick up something."

Steve tucked the passbook into his shirt pocket. "I'll keep what you said in mind, Mungo." He lifted his hand in a good-bye wave and walked out. He wanted to tell Dixon that he had put the money in a safe place as Dixon suggested. Steve scowled unhappily. Having money raised one problem after another. Now North's advice would be clanging in his head like a great clarion bell.

He walked slowly down the street until, four blocks from Dixon's office, he saw a crowd of people. He elbowed his way to the center of the crowd; anger at his rough passage faded when they saw who it was.

"What's the trouble here?" Steve snapped. He saw the body lying on the ground, and he didn't have to ask any more questions. There had been violence here, and not too long ago, for the blood still had a bright color. The victim had been stabbed in the belly, and a vicious stroke of the blade had opened him up like a fish being prepared for a meal.

Steve looked hard-eyed at the crowd. "Who saw this?" He looked at one face after another, and each looked uneasily away. "Come on," Steve barked. "Surely some of you saw what happened."

A man raised his hand reluctantly. "I saw it, Deputy," he admitted. "They were just coming out of the saloon over there." He jerked a thumb at the saloon across the street. "They were arguing over something. I was too far away to hear what it was. Then this one"—he looked at the body—"knocked the other one down. He hit a smaller man, but that man was faster than anything I ever saw. He bounded to his feet with a knife in his hand. He came in fast and opened up this one's belly." Another look at the body. "He didn't have the slightest idea it was coming."

Steve waved his hand impatiently. All this was fine, and he had a witness. But what he wanted were names or at least descriptions.

"Did you know him?"

The man he questioned shook his head. "Never saw either of them before. The man with the knife took off on a dead run down the street. Ain't seen him since the fight." He looked around for corroboration, and several heads nodded.

Steve didn't doubt any of that. "Some of you stay here and watch him. I'm going by to tell Andrews to pick him up."

He nodded curtly to the crowd and left. He heard them muttering behind him. Right now violent death had its sobering effect. That effect wouldn't last much longer than it took Andrews to pick up the corpse.

Steve stopped in at the undertaker's, and Andrews' eyes were apprehensive. "Not another one," he muttered. "Do you realize that makes twelve bodies I've picked up this month? It's getting so that every time you come in, I know what to expect."

Steve grinned stiffly at him. "You complaining about good business?"

"Not as good as it sounds," Andrews replied querulously. "I had to bury six of those unfortunates at my own expense. Another unknown body? No known relations?"

Steve shook his head. "I'm afraid so."

Andrews moaned in protest.

"Maybe we're both in the wrong business," Steve said. He shook his head at the puzzled frown on Andrews' face. There was no use trying to explain to him. Andrews was getting sick at certain aspects of his business, just as Steve was getting sick of his job.

Steve scowled as he walked down the street. He was becoming a harbinger of death.

CHAPTER 21

CLEATIS cleaned the last stall and added another load to the growing pile of manure at the back of the big corral. He cleaned out the wheelbarrow and restored it to its proper place. He put away the pitchfork and approached Jorman, who had fallen asleep in his chair and didn't hear him.

Cleatis stood silent, looking at him. He didn't resent Jorman falling asleep while he had to work. That was Jorman's privilege. He owned the place. Linus used to fall asleep often, and Cleatis had never resented it. He cleared his throat, and Jorman heard the sound, or else eyes watching him dug through the fog of sleep.

Jorman opened his eyes and looked wildly about him. "What is it, Cleatis?" His annoyance showed. He didn't like anybody sneaking up on him.

"I finished the stalls, Mr. Jorman. Is there anything else you want me to do?"

"You couldn't have finished." Jorman's surprise showed. "I didn't expect you to finish today."

"It's all done. Come and see."

Jorman heaved himself out of the chair and followed Cleatis down the row of stalls. "I'll be damned." He repeated the oath at each stall. "As slick as a whistle." He had hired himself a prize. He hadn't seen such a thorough job in the past six months.

"That'll be enough for today, Cleatis. Take the rest of the day off." He fished in his pocket for a dollar bill. "Take it. You've earned it. Go out and have your supper."

Cleatis followed Jorman back to the head of the runway. "I don't feel right, stopping so soon. Feels like I haven't earned my money."

"You earned it. Doesn't paying you that extra prove it?

You can get a pretty good meal at Emma's place. She's down the street a couple of blocks."

He started to add something when a customer walked into the runway. "Get my horse, will you, Holt?"

"Sure, Marshal. Be right back with him."

Cleatis was aware the marshal looked him over thoroughly. He kept looking at the ground. A quiver started within him. Could this be the marshal he had come so far to find?

Jorman came back with the horse and handed over the reins. "Expect to be gone long, Marshal?"

"Should be back around dark," Dixon replied. He swung up, then looked down at Jorman. "New boy you hired, Holt?"

"The best one I ever hired," Jorman said enthusiastically. "He did as much work as all the others put together."

"Glad to hear that. Oklahoma City can use a lot more of that kind." He nodded to Jorman, and his gaze at Cleatis wasn't so sharp and penetrating.

Cleatis waited until he was out of sight. "I heard you call him Marshal, Mr. Jorman. Is he somebody famous?"

"He sure is. You haven't been here long enough to hear about Marshal Sam Dixon. He's made many a criminal sorry he was ever assigned to this district."

The quiver had grown into the lashing of a savage whip. There went one of the men Linus had sent him after. He wished there was some way he could tell Linus to quit his fretting. Half of the job would be done before this night was over.

"Why don't you go out and get your supper, Cleatis? Emma serves a good meal for fifty cents." He started away, then stopped as a thought hit him. "I wouldn't wander too long around town. It can be a rough place after dark."

"I intend coming back right after I eat," Cleatis replied. "If you haven't got anything else for me to do, I might turn in. I'm kinda tuckered out."

"You do that," Jorman said heartily. "After the day you put in, you got every right to be tired. If I'm not around when you get back, go ahead and turn in. Nothing left I can't handle."

He watched Cleatis leave, his eyes warm. Funny thing about help. It came in assorted packages, very few marked "excellent." Jorman chortled to himself. He had one of those marked "excellent."

Cleatis found Emma's with no trouble. The rush of business would have marked it for him. He had to wait a half hour before he was served, but to a patient man that wasn't a long time.

Emma had a half-dozen women serving tables. One of them came up to Cleatis and gave him a friendly smile. "You're new here, aren't you?"

Cleatis looked at her with a degree of alarm. "No," he mumbled. "I been here a long time."

The waitress shrugged. This customer didn't want a friendly approach. She wasn't complaining. After some of the remarks and the pawing the male customers gave her, it was a relief to find a withdrawn one. This big man was frowning over the hastily scrawled menu. It could be that he was having trouble reading the poor writing. Emma didn't write a good hand. She had seen other men struggling to decipher the menu.

"I can recommend the stew, mister," she volunteered. "Twenty-five cents a bowl. All you can eat for forty cents." By the way his face cleared, her guess about his difficulty with the writing was correct.

"That'll be just fine," he said, handing the menu back. "I'll have the forty-cent portion."

She started to tell him that very few men were able to handle that much stew, then looking at his size, decided the advice might be wrong. She glanced at him several times while she waited for the stew to be ladled up. Something was on this one's mind. She could tell by the way his eyes glittered and the fixed set of his face. He looked almost angry, and a little shiver ran through her. She would hate to have one like this after her. By his dress and manners, he was from the country. She shrugged. She had no interest in a yokel anyway.

She brought the bowl of stew to his table and set it before him. She placed a plate of bread beside it, then added a small dish of butter. His eyes grew rounder and rounder as he watched her.

"Do I get all this?" he asked in awe.

She nodded brightly. "You finish this bowl, and I'll bring you another. I'll get your coffee."

Cleatis fell to eating with gusto. The stew was good, with thick chunks of meat and potatoes swimming in a thick gravy. It was fascinating watching him put the food away. By the time the waitress returned with his coffee, the bowl was nearly empty. The plate of bread was gone, too.

She laughed. "You were hungry. I might as well refill everything."

Cleatis nodded. "I'd sure appreciate that."

He was waiting when she returned with another bowl of stew, bread and butter. How this man could eat. She guessed it took a lot of fuel to keep this big engine going.

"More?" she asked, as he used a half slice of bread to wipe his bowl clean.

Cleatis belched and shook his head. "I think that'll do, ma'am."

She should think so. She didn't know of another man in town who could put away this much food. Cleatis paid his bill and thanked her.

He nodded at Jorman as he passed him at the entrance of the stable. "Going to turn in, if you don't mind, Holt."

"You go right ahead," Jorman said heartily.

Cleatis retired to the tackroom. It was close enough to the stable's entrance that he could see everybody who came in. He had no idea how long he would have to wait for the marshal.

He picked up the rifle from a corner of the tackroom and thrust its barrel down his pant leg, the stock reaching under the bib of his overalls. He took a few tentative steps. The muzzle just reached to his knee. It wasn't going to hamper his walking. He could move about without anybody noticing the rifle. He returned to his vigil, and his eagerness burned like a flame.

Marshal Dixon had said he would be back around dark, but he was later. It was full night before he rode through the entrance.

Cleatis, peering through a crack in the boards, said a soft "Ah" at the sight of him.

The marshal threw off and handed the reins to Jorman. They exchanged a few words. Cleatis waited patiently. He didn't care how long the talk lasted; sooner or later, Dixon would go.

Dixon finally nodded, then turned to leave. Jorman led the horse deeper into the stable. Cleatis waited a moment longer, then slipped out of the tackroom. It was close to the entrance, and only a few steps from the street. He kept close to the building when he stepped outside. Satisfaction swelled up within him again. The marshal was going down the street less than a half block ahead.

Cleatis fell in behind him. Dixon moved with a limp that noticeably slowed him down, and it wasn't hard to keep him in sight. For a big man, Cleatis moved with an ease that was as fluid as flowing water. He wouldn't make his attempt here, not while the street was so crowded.

Dixon turned off on a side street, and after he left the crowded business district, the traffic faded away until only an occasional person came by. Each was absorbed in his own thoughts, and none of them paid any attention to Cleatis. Twice, Dixon stopped and glanced back. Luck was with Cleatis. He anticipated the movement, for he was in a motionless position each time Dixon glanced back. Cleatis blended well with the deep shadows.

Now was as good a time as any, he decided. The longer he waited, the more uncertain he would be that more people wouldn't pass this way. He moved with a faster pace, cutting the distance between him and Dixon to less than fifty yards. Even with this poor light, Cleatis had a good target.

He pulled the rifle out of his overalls. It was already loaded, and he cocked it. He paused and snugged the rifle butt against his shoulder. This time, Dixon must have really sensed something, for he stopped and partially turned.

Cleatis centered Dixon in the gun's sights and squeezed the trigger. The bark of the rifle was loud, but Dixon never made a sound. He threw up his arms, half spun, then slumped as though he didn't have a bone in his body.

Cleatis nodded with satisfaction. This was the first man he'd ever shot, but he had seen game fall. He knew the unmistakable stamp of death.

He slipped the rifle back under his overalls, and scurrying between a row of tents, cut across the city. Now he had to work his way back to the stable and slip undetected into the tackroom.

CHAPTER 22

STEVE glanced worriedly at the clock. It was nearing ten, and Dixon still hadn't returned. Had he run into trouble? There was always that possibility with a lawman. Steve had put off his rounds of the town, hoping to see Dixon return safely.

Steve sighed and rose. Well, he'd better get at it. He hadn't reached the door when a man burst through it, his eyes wide, his mouth open and spluttering.

"Easy, Wirt," Steve said. "You look like something is chasing you." Wirt was in his sixties, always hanging around the office. He admired lawmen and was always available to run errands.

Wirt gulped hard and made a minor recovery. "I just stumbled over a body, Steve," he said in a shaky voice.

Steve's eyes turned alert. It must be somebody important to make Wirt this agitated. "Do you know who it is, Wirt?"

"I sure do," Wirt said in a hollow voice. "I turned him over. It's Marshal Dixon."

Steve felt as though he had been hit on the head by a club. His tongue wouldn't move, and the sounds he made were hardly human. "Are you sure, Wirt?" he finally managed to gasp.

Wirt looked sorrowfully at him. He knew the close bond between Steve and the marshal. "There ain't no doubt of it, Steve."

"Where?" Steve demanded.

"About a block from here."

Steve scowled at the information. Shouldn't he have heard a shot? He couldn't blame himself too much for negligence. Guns were being fired every hour all over town. If he had heard the shot, it had no particular meaning to him.

"Take me to him, Wirt," he said in a barely audible voice. His eyes were beginning to sting as they walked the block. He fiercely fought the welling tears. He didn't want to break down and bawl like a baby.

"There," Wirt said, pointing ahead.

Steve had already seen the dark, huddled mass of a body on the ground. "Maybe he's still alive," he said, grabbing at the faintest of chances.

Wirt shook his head. "He ain't. I checked good before I reported to you."

Steve dropped to his knees beside the body. Tears ran down his cheeks, and he didn't give a damn if anybody saw him. This man meant a lot to him. He had given him a start and a purpose in life. Why, only earlier this evening, they had been talking about the dangers of a lawman's life.

The light wasn't good, but Steve could make out the mass of a dark stain on Dixon's side. At a guess, Steve would say that he was just turning as the shot got him. Had somebody called to him? Steve would give anything for the answer to that.

He was silent for so long that Wirt asked uneasily, "Are you all right, Steve?"

"I'm all right," Steve said in a dead voice.

"Is he dead?"

"He's dead," Steve said grimly. He had bent close and listened for Dixon's breathing. There was none.

Wirt asked the question that was tearing Steve apart. "Who do you think did it, Steve?"

It took the greatest effort to keep from yelling at him. "I wish I knew," he managed to say in a fairly quiet tone. "I could pick out two dozen men in this town who would like to see Sam dead."

There was a helpless note in Wirt's voice. "How are you going to go about finding him?"

If Wirt didn't shut up, he was going to drive Steve crazy with his questions. "I'll look around in the morning, Wirt. Can't see anything now."

He straightened, his face stolid. All the hurt was inside; his belly ached from the loss. "Wirt, will you help me carry Sam down to Andrews?"

"Won't he come down here and pick him up?"

That was an unwise question. It unleashed all the rage in Steve. "Goddamn it," he panted. "You want to let him lie here in the dust? He never turned down a request you made."

Wirt shook his head. "Forget I said that, Steve. This shook me up so much, I wasn't thinking."

Steve nodded acceptance of the explanation. He could appreciate how Wirt felt. Hell, his own thoughts were churning so that he couldn't get ahold of a thing. He let Wirt have Dixon's feet, thinking it would be the lighter part of the load. Steve tried to keep from staring down at the dead face as they carried Dixon along.

They picked up the usual curious crowd. Every step of the burdened trip seemed to draw more of the morbidly curious. They pressed in closer, hampering Steve's and Wirt's progress.

"Goddamn it, get back," Steve yelled fiercely. That pushed them back a little, but before long they were crowding in again.

Andrews met them at the door. "I saw the crowd," he said in a tight voice. "Who is it this time?"

Wirt and Steve carried Dixon into the building. "Slam the door in their faces," Steve said furiously. He helped Wirt carry Dixon to a table in that bleak back room. He already had too much familiarity with it.

"What happened?" Andrews asked, pulling at his fingers.

"Some bastard gunned him down," Steve said in a strained voice. "I doubt Sam even knew what hit him."

Andrews pulled harder at his fingers. "What's going to happen to all of us now, Steve? Who's going to protect us?"

Steve looked him over with a jaundiced eye. "You know, I don't think Sam gives a damn about that now." He didn't stop, nor did he turn his head at Andrews' little bleat.

"What'll I do with him?" Andrews cried.

"You know more about that than I do," Steve replied sardonically. "Get him ready for burial. I'll be back in the morning."

Wirt was shaking when they got outside. "I feel like I'm falling apart," he said mournfully.

"Yes," Steve acknowledged. "Go on back to the office. There's a bottle in the lower right-hand drawer of the desk. Pull on it. It'll quiet you down. I've got something to do."

Wirt didn't want to be left alone, and it showed in his face. "What are you going to do?"

"I've got to wire Colonel Jones at Muskogee what's happened."

Wirt nodded. He knew Jones' responsibility as head marshal for the Judicial District of Kansas. "I thought he was in Kansas, Steve."

Steve shook his head. "The last I heard of him, he was in Muskogee."

"Maybe he'll appoint you marshal for Oklahoma City," Wirt ventured.

"I wouldn't have the damned job as a gift," Steve said savagely. He turned away. He didn't want to talk further about this.

Mosley, the night operator, was on duty at the depot when Steve arrived. Steve wrote out a long wire and growled, "Get this off as fast as you can."

"Sure, Steve," Mosley said. He was busy reading Steve's writing as Steve turned away. Mosley didn't know about Dixon's killing yet. He would before he read much farther.

Steve was a half-dozen steps away when Mosley called out a startled, "Hey."

Steve looked back. "It's all there. Just get it off." He lengthened his stride. He didn't want to talk to anybody.

Quite a crowd gathered for Dixon's funeral. Many people didn't like him, but a far greater number liked and respected him. Steve's face looked as though it were carved from granite. He had to keep it that way for fear he would break down openly. He stared straight ahead, his body rigid, his eyes squinched to keep the moisture from spilling out.

The preacher droned on and on, eulogizing Sam Dixon. He recounted all his days as a lawman, then pointed out that many persons here might owe their very lives to the marshal.

Would the long-winded old fool ever stop? Steve was on the verge of protesting loudly. He knew all these things the preacher was saying.

The dissertation finally ended, and the crowd began to drift away. Steve heard their chatter, and a few of them laughed over something. A man's life was over, wrapped up in those bleak moments. Steve plunged ahead. He didn't want anybody trying to talk to him.

The preacher caught up with him. He was a scrawny little man with a serious, absorbed face. "Did I do all right, Steve?" he asked anxiously.

"What do you want? Credit?" Steve asked in a suppressed voice. "What did you really do? You said a few words over a dead man. Do you think those words helped Sam, or anybody who listened to you?"

The preacher's face reddened. "Here now," he spluttered. "There's no call for that kind of talk."

"Maybe there is," Steve said grimly. If he had deflated the preacher's ego, he wasn't apologizing. Couldn't this preacher see that the living needed comfort too?

Steve walked back to the office, and for several moments he couldn't stop his pacing. Everywhere he looked he saw Dixon. He could almost imagine he heard him speak. How familiar the old scenes were, and they kept rolling back on him. "Oh goddamn it, Sam. I'm sorry." His lips trembled, but no sound came out.

He sat down in Dixon's chair and looked in the desk. He hoped Wirt hadn't killed that bottle. The only thing Steve could see that would bring him relief was to get roaring drunk. The bottle was still in the desk drawer, and Steve blew out a breath. Wirt hadn't needed much to calm him down. Steve tilted the bottle up and let the liquor run down his throat.

"Do you think that's going to help you, Steve?" that familiar voice asked mockingly. It was so real that Steve was startled. He could swear it was Dixon speaking.

"It'll help," Steve muttered. He didn't know what else he could do. He had spent the early-morning hours carefully going over the ground where Dixon was killed. He hadn't found anything revealing. Oh he had found some scuffed-up footsteps, but they didn't tell him a thing. Those footprints were made by booted feet, but 90 per cent of the people in Oklahoma City wore boots. He had found a single spent rifle shell. The dust had piled up against it, almost obscuring it. He bounced the spent cartridge in his palm. It was equally unrevealing. It was a popular caliber, and he could probably find a thousand rifles in this town that used the same ammunition.

Recalling the fruitless morning brought back all the crushing frustration. "Oh goddamn it," he yelled. He tilted

the bottle up again. He lowered it and scrubbed the back
of his hand across his mouth. "I'll find him, Sam," he
whispered. He didn't see how he could do that. At the moment, it seemed an impossible task. But, somehow, he
would find Sam's killer.

CHAPTER 23

CLEATIS hammered lustily at the loose boards on a stall.
He finished nailing one board and moved to the next stall.
"That stallion sure kicked the hell out of this stall," he
said over his shoulder.

Jorman shook his head in wonder. This man sure was a
worker. Jorman had thought Cleatis would appreciate the
time off to go to Dixon's funeral, but Cleatis could hardly
wait to return to the stable.

"Cleatis, you make me feel like a slave driver," he protested. "I wanted you to take the whole afternoon off."

"Getting too far behind," Cleatis said. "Besides, that funeral didn't mean anything to me."

Jorman looked pained. "I'd say you were the only one
who felt that way. It meant a lot to everybody there. I
thought Steve Truman would break into pieces. I pointed
him out to you."

Cleatis kept his head turned so that Jorman couldn't see
the savage glow in his eyes. "That tall, thin one?" he
asked. He would never forget Truman's face. This was the
one who had actually killed Elmer. Dixon had only directed him. Cleatis would know a far greater satisfaction when
he evened up the score for that murder.

"Dixon and Truman have done a lot for Oklahoma
City," Jorman said.

Cleatis grunted in answer. Anything he said right now
might reveal his true feelings about those two. Oh God, he
wished Linus knew how well he had done. Linus would

swell with pride. But Linus would have to wait until he returned home. He gathered up his saw and hammer and loose boards and moved on to the next stall. "Thought I saw some loose boards on this one."

Jorman shook his had. "I give up on you, Cleatis. Never saw a man so swallowed up by his work." He grinned broadly. "I'm not complaining. I know how lucky I am that you stopped by here."

Almost a week had passed since Steve sent the telegram. He was beginning to believe he would never receive an answer. Every time he stepped into this office, he saw Sam Dixon again. He wanted to be relieved from this job as soon as possible. Oh he did the work demanded of him; he made his rounds, he tried to keep law and order, but his heart wasn't in it.

Steve turned back toward the office, and the dread of going into it again was stronger than ever. The paperwork was piling up on him, since Dixon had always done most of it. Steve gritted his teeth. He had asked for relief. Weren't the higher authorities going to grant his wishes?

A voice hailed him, and Steve looked around for the speaker.

Mungo North crossed hastily to him. "Steve," he said, extending his hand, "how are things going?" At the bleakness settling across Steve's face, North apologized. "Sorry I said that. Terrible about what happened to Sam."

"Yes," Steve said tersely. His tone warned North not to continue with the subject.

North had keen perception, for he caught that tone immediately. "Do you have a few minutes to spend this morning, Steve? I have something I want to show you." He led Steve down the street some three blocks, stopped, and said a triumphant, "There."

Steve looked in puzzlement in the direction of the pointing finger. He didn't see anything but a relatively new building. "I don't see what you mean, Mungo."

North made an impatient gesture. "There! The hardware store."

Steve's frown didn't ease. He didn't see why the store should mean anything to him.

North was excited. "Kirby Lewis built that building. It's one of the better ones in town."

Steve could grant that. The building was of wood, and

from this distance looked firmly constructed. He could see the sign "Lewis Hardware" on the window. He still couldn't see why he should have any interest in this structure.

"Oh Lord, are you blind?" North asked disgustedly. "Lewis put too much money in that building, then understocked his store. As a result, he's not doing much business. He made a tentative offer to me of twenty-five hundred dollars. It could be a real buy. Poor management more than anything is putting Lewis out of business."

Steve thought of paying for Dixon's funeral. "I haven't got twenty-five hundred," he stated.

North's mouth sagged. "Oh God! You haven't spent all that money, have you?"

Steve's lips twitched at North's agitation. "I spent a hundred dollars of it. I paid for Sam's funeral."

North's face cleared. "I thought you'd gotten rid of all or most of it in some wild spending spree. I think Lewis could be talked into taking less. The last I heard, he was being pressed hard." His eyes danced. "Want to talk to him about it?"

Dixon's death had put the final twist in Steve's determination to get this badge off his chest. "Mungo, do you think a man could make a living out of that store?"

"I know he could. Kirby ran a sloppy store. The tighter business got, the nastier he got with his customers. He ran away more business than a hard-working man could ever draw. Don't offer him the price he's asking. Offer him two thousand. I think he'll snap it up. That'll leave you some capital to restock. Do you want to talk to him now?"

Steve drew a deep breath. He wanted to get out of the law-enforcement business. This might be just the road he was looking for.

Lewis looked at the pair with open disfavor. He hadn't shaved in several days, and his shirt was filthy. "What do you want?" he growled.

Steve looked about the store. The floor hadn't been swept in weeks, and the aisles were cluttered. Every bin was jammed with an assortment of merchandise. Steve wondered how Lewis ever found anything.

"Kirby," North said, "you mentioned to me yesterday that you'd be willing to sell out, if you found a buyer. Do you still feel that way?"

Lewis spit a gob of tobacco juice on the floor. Steve felt

a stab of annoyance. This was almost like the man was spitting on his floor.

"I'd sell out," Lewis growled. "Man breaks his back and nothing comes from it."

North turned to Steve. "It's up to you, Steve."

Steve felt shaky inside. He had never owned anything as big as this before. He had never even run a store. It scared him to think of all the pitfalls that could be lurking ahead of him.

"I'll offer you two thousand dollars," he said firmly.

"Twenty-four hundred," Lewis countered.

"Two thousand," Steve said adamantly.

Lewis made one more pass. "Twenty-three hundred."

Steve turned to leave, though it was the hardest thing he ever did. "Two thousand," he said over his shoulder. "Coming, North?"

Lewis made a frantic grab for Steve's arm. "All cash?"

"Cash," Steve said.

"Done," Lewis growled. "This place's been nothing but a royal pain. I'll be glad to get rid of it."

Steve kept the elation off his face. He wanted to throw back his head and howl. He was the newest businessman in Oklahoma City. "Mungo, can you see that all the papers are ready by morning. I'll meet you at the bank in the morning." He walked out, his head held high in pride.

North nudged him with an elbow. "You look like a kid who still believes in Santa Claus."

Steve threw back his head and let the laughter roll. "Maybe I do, Mungo."

"I don't think you'll ever regret it, Steve," North said earnestly. "Run properly, this place can be a gold mine."

"It'll be run properly."

North whacked Steve on the back. "I don't have any doubt of it, Steve."

They parted at the next corner, and Steve continued on to the marshal's office. Damn it, how he wanted his replacement to hurry and get here. Mentally and spiritually, Steve was no longer a lawman. He owned a hardware store.

He stepped inside the office, and for an instant his heart jumped into his throat. A man sat at Dixon's desk, his back turned, his eyes fixed on the outdoors. He and Dixon were similar in build, and for a terrible instant, Steve had the feeling that Dixon had returned and was sitting in his old spot. He savagely raked that impression out of his head.

"Yes?" Steve said coldly.

The man whirled at the sound of his voice, and Steve caught the reflection of light from his badge. He really didn't look anything like Dixon. This man was younger, and there was no similarity in the faces. This one's features were cut on craggier lines, and the mouth was larger. But there was the same cold glint in the eyes, and this man had the same general appearance of competence that Dixon had.

"I'm Dan Daniels," the man said. "Colonel Jones sent me."

"Steve Truman. You the new marshal?" Steve asked.

"That's my purpose. Any objections?"

"No, of course not," Steve replied, and there was compliance in his tone. "But it took you a lot longer to get here than I expected."

Daniels squinted at him. "Sounds like you're fed up with your job."

Steve grinned wryly. "I am. I was just waiting for you to get here before I handed in my badge."

"Ah," Daniels said knowingly. "The same old feeling that hits all of us every now and then. Happen to you when Sam was killed?"

Steve had started thinking about resigning at the finding of Sally's body. Sam's killing was the final straw. "Partially," he acknowledged.

"Sit down," Daniels invited. "I'd like to hear a little about Sam. We served together some twenty years ago. In fact, I talked with him about the advisability of going into the new territory. I warned him that it was going to be a rough country."

"You knew what you were talking about," Steve said flatly.

Daniels nodded. "Happens every time a law officer goes into an uncivilized land. I had second thoughts when I was offered this new post. I thought it over and finally decided to accept."

"I'm glad you did. I can't get out of here quick enough."

"You got something in mind?"

They spoke the same language, they thought alike. Daniels was easy to talk to. "I have," Steve replied. "I just bought a hardware business." There was a challenge in his eyes.

"I always hate to see a good lawman quit," Daniels said reflectively. "And you sure were one of those." He grinned whimsically at Steve's reaction. "Your reputation gets around. I heard about you when I worked in Arkansas." He sighed. "That was a pleasant district. The country was old enough to settle down. Then I've got to stick my nose into a mess like this." A soft sigh puffed out his lips. "Do you know what you want?"

"You don't think I'll make it in business?" The challenge was still in Steve's tone.

"Hey now. I didn't say that at all. Other men have made successes out of new businesses. You will too. I'm not saying it's going to be easy. But you'll make it. You've got that look."

Steve relaxed. Daniels wasn't criticizing him. "I'm sure as hell going to try."

Daniels' eyes had a faraway look. "When I look back, I think I went wrong in hanging onto this tinware. Now I'm too old to even think of doing something else."

They saw there in a pleasant, companionable silence. "I'll tell you one way to make a sure success out of your business," Daniels finally said.

"What's that?" Steve asked lazily.

"Get a good woman. With a good woman behind a man, he can't miss."

Steve chuckled. "I don't even know that kind of woman. The only ones I know hardly fit that description."

Daniels nodded. "I know. I was young once. I knew that kind too. You know, I can't even remember their faces." He stood and walked over to a lamp. He removed the globe and struck a match to the wick.

"Is it getting dark so soon?" Steve asked in mild surprise. He hadn't noticed the darkness creeping up on them.

"Good conversation eats away the time," Daniels said and grinned.

Steve heaved himself to his feet. "I've gotta be going."

"I'll tell you another thing you're doing," Daniels said.

"What's that?"

"You're taking your neck off the block. There'll be no half-crazy outlaw trying to collect it."

Those sober words brought back all the talk between Steve and Dixon. Dixon had recognized what Daniels was saying, but Steve hadn't done anything about it. In an instant, it was too late.

"I hope you're right," Steve said. He unpinned the badge from his shirt and laid it on the desk. "It's been a pleasure talking to you."

"The same," Daniels replied. He had a good grip, hard and positive, but then, Dixon had had the same kind of a grip.

"Any money due you, Steve?"

"Only a few days. Not enough to sweat over."

"Just the same, you've got it coming. I'll see that it's sent here. Will you be dropping by in a few days?"

Steve had no desire to ever see the inside of this office again. Too many old memories were tied up here. But Daniels was trying to do him a favor. There was no sense slamming the offer back in his teeth.

"One of these days," he said, and moved toward the door. He stepped outside, and an eerie little feeling ran through him. Maybe it was what Daniels said about a lawman putting his neck on the block. A new fence running for a full two lots was just across the street. Steve had watched its construction for the past couple of days. He had been intending to walk over there and see what required a fence of that height. Other things had occupied his mind, and he'd never gotten around to it. That would be an ideal spot for someone to lay in ambush for him. Steve swore at himself. That was pure fantasy.

He moved along, keeping a wary eye on the fence. A little inner voice kept tormenting him. "What if some of the old boys who have every reason to dislike you are still alive?" it mocked him.

"Oh, hell," he said in disgust. A man could build the damnedest specters out of his imagination.

But that damned little squeamish feeling wouldn't go away. The sweat was beginning to stand out on his skin, and it prickled. "Oh Jesus," he muttered in self-disgust. "You're letting your imagination run away with you." Just the same, he kept an alert eye on the fence. He didn't know what good that would do him, but he couldn't take his eyes off that fence.

He didn't see the tin can directly before his boot. His foot came down on it, and it rolled under his weight, throwing him forward. He went down hard, his outthrust forearms breaking the force of his fall.

Another thought didn't have time to form in his mind when the report of a rifle echoed through the air. He heard the bullet smashing into a wall behind him. He didn't actually feel the passage of the bullet, but he had the sinking sensation that it had been close.

Sam was killed in a similar manner, he thought dismally. He thought he heard the pound of running feet, coming from behind that fence. He didn't have time to investigate; he was too busy rolling away from the possibility of another shot.

CHAPTER 24

THE wall stopped him. He rolled up against it, and was filled with a frantic fear that he couldn't escape. He got his feet under him and stood, drawing his pistol at the same time. He heard no further sound of activity across the street; then the skin of his neck tightened, and he whipped about as he heard the pound of running feet.

"Steve," a voice called, "are you all right?"

For an instant, Steve had been fearful of an attack from another direction. The voice wiped out that possibility. That was Daniels, running as hard as he could out of the office.

Daniels came up to him, his face taut. "Steve, I heard a shot, didn't I?"

"You did," Steve replied, his voice not quite steady. "Somebody was waiting for me behind that fence. He cut down on me."

Daniels swore furiously. "Any idea who it was?"

"I didn't even get a glimpse of him. But I thought I heard somebody running." He scowled at Daniels. "One thing bothers me: Why didn't he take another shot? I was pretty helpless, rolling around on the ground. I stepped on a can and fell." A little shiver ran through him. "I don't want anybody ever coming any closer."

"Let's go across the street and see what we can find," Daniels suggested.

"The gate's at the far end of the fence. I watched it being built. I don't know why it was built."

"Someone wanted a lot of privacy," Daniels said. He thought for a moment, then muttered, "Naw. It couldn't be."

"What couldn't be?"

"I got the notion that the ambusher built the fence to hide behind. But that'd be too much work and expense. The fence was just there. Your would-be assassin used it."

Steve nodded. He unlatched the gate and opened it. The hinges squeaked as he and Daniels walked through it.

"Pretty dark to find anything," Steve said dispiritedly.

"Probably," Daniels agreed. "But we might pick up something that would give us a clue. Stick close to the fence. I'd say he was right up against it."

Daniels moved a slow step at a time, never more than a foot or two from the fence. He was halfway down the fence when he muttered an oath.

"Find something?" Steve called.

"Maybe," Daniels grunted. "Don't walk here." He was down on his hands and knees, peering at the ground. "Damned darkness," he complained. He struck a match, and the fence protected the feeble flame from the wind. "I thought I saw something," he said triumphantly.

The match burned down, and Daniels swore and dropped it. He lit another and held it close to the impression in the ground.

"Somebody stood here," he said. "A big-footed, heavy man. Look at the size of that print. His weight really packed the ground." He straightened and examined the fence. "Hah! I thought so. He used this knothole." He struck another match. "Yes, there're powder burns around that hole. This hole was barely big enough to stick his gun muzzle through."

He dropped back to his knees and made another search of the ground at the base of the fence. "Here it is." Immense satisfaction was in his voice. He straightened and handed the shell to Steve.

Steve turned the shell over in his hand, his expression grim.

"Does it tell you anything?" Daniels asked.

"Not much. I think it's the same caliber used on Sam." Steve grimaced. "I'm looking for a big-footed man with no face. He uses a rifle."

"Maybe a single shot," Daniels mused. "That could be the reason why there were no more shots. Can you name anybody who hates you and Sam enough to want to kill you?"

"Nobody that I can think of. I know one thing for sure: He's still out there."

"He doesn't know you've quit your job," Daniels said reflectively. "When he hears that, it might cool him off."

Steve shook his head. "Whatever set him after me in the first place is still chewing on him." His face was unhappy, and that tight, twisting knot was back in his belly again.

"Yes," Daniels agreed. "It's too dark to pick up anything more. I'll be back in the morning to see if I can find something. Watch yourself, Steve."

"Sure," Steve growled. That helpless feeling was seizing him again. He didn't even know what he was looking for.

He stood in the middle of the hardware store, looking for a place to start. He had signed the necessary papers this morning, and given Lewis the cash. Steve was glad to see that sour face leave. Lewis had gotten on his nerves with his constant bellyaching.

Steve looked around again, the dismay spreading over his face. This was a pigpen, not a store. Before he could reopen for business, he had to sweep this place out and put some order into the bins and shelves. He was fortunate in one respect: He had almost every tool or implement he could need to clean this place up.

Steve discarded the idea of sweeping the length of the floor, then pushing the dirt on out the door. That would be the quickest way, but it would be slovenly. No, he better block out a small area, work on it slowly and carefully until he was satisfied it was thoroughly clean.

He mentally lined out a five-foot square. His irritation rose as he swept. Good Lord! It didn't look as though Lewis had ever swept this place. Steve shook his head as he looked at the accumulated pile of dirt and trash. It didn't seem possible that a space that small could contain so much dirt. Steve swept the dirt into a box, then carried the box outdoors. He dumped it in the street, ducking his head as the dust rose.

"I could do that for you, mister."

Steve whipped his head around at the words. A kid not over fifteen years old was watching him, bright-eyed. The freckles dusting his face gave it an appealing look.

"I'm looking for a job," the kid said earnestly. "I stopped here before, but Mr. Lewis wouldn't listen to me." He spread his hands. "Looks like the place could stand a good cleaning."

Steve grinned. This was an observant kid. "It sure could. Mr. Lewis is no longer the owner. I'm the new owner."

The boy's eyes widened. "Then maybe you could use some help. I'd work good. While I was sweeping out, you could be straightening things in the store."

Steve thought of those cluttered bins. Lewis had thrown tools and materials indiscriminately into the bins. "We might work out something," Steve said solemnly. "What kind of wages would you expect?"

The boy's whoop of joy showed there was still a lot of kid in him. "I'd leave that up to you, sir. Whatever you think is right."

Steve handed him the box. "We'll start at fifty cents a day until we see how you work out. Then we might bump that some." The boy bounded ahead of him, and Steve called him back. "I ought to know your name."

That bright, engaging face turned toward Steve. "Jimmy Rollins, sir."

"I'm Steve—"

Before he could finish, Jimmy interrupted. "I know who you are. You're Steve Truman. Everybody in town knows you." His eyes glowed. "Can I call you Steve?"

Steve chuckled. "That's what all my friends call me." Maybe this was an omen of how this business was going to turn out. He had hired a smart, willing kid, and if his business turned out half as well, his venture was going to do all right.

He showed Jimmy what he had been doing. "Take a small patch at a time. Don't move until you're sure it's clean."

"Yes, sir," Jimmy said eagerly. He grabbed the broom and made the dust fly.

Steve choked against the rising clouds. "Don't rush it,"

he cautioned. "You'll burn yourself out and won't have anything left for the rest of the day."

"Yeah," Jimmy said sagely. "And I'm raising the dust from the floor to settle over everything."

Steve grinned. This was one smart kid. They were going to get along.

Steve moved to his task of trying to straighten out the bins. That damned Lewis had stuffed a bin full without trying to keep the tools sorted. He had hammers and chisels crammed in with saws and braces and bits. Steve's frown grew as he sorted out the tools. He didn't know much about tools, but this was a hell of a way to treat them.

He was kneeling before a bin behind the counter when he heard somebody say, "Anybody here?"

His mouth dropped open. He could swear that sounded like Sally. He shook his head. He knew that couldn't be, but for an instant, the impression had swept over him. He rose to his full height. On the other side of the counter a woman stood, her back toward him as she looked about the store.

From the back she had a trim figure, and the feeling of knowing her returned. Sally had looked like this. This woman's hair was reddish, and it flowed down to the nape of her neck, where it curled softly. For a moment, the vividness of the impression scared Steve. But that was a fantasy of the wildest kind.

He cleared his throat. "Yes, ma'am?"

The woman whirled, her face startled. "I didn't know you were anywhere near."

She had the same coloring as Sally and was about the same height. Her figure was youthful, but of course she was several years older. Her features didn't have Sally's soft immaturity, and her eyes were green where Sally's had been blue.

He realized he was staring, and he colored. She was aware of his staring too, for her eyes darkened. He gulped. His breathing was coming harder, and his heart was beginning to pound. Oh Lord, he had never looked at a woman so beautiful.

"For a moment, I thought you were someone else," he apologized. "The resemblance is so strong that it shook me."

Her face cleared, and her eyes resumed their normal

shade. Her laughter was natural. "I hope that's a compliment."

"It is," he assured her. "Now, what can I do for you?"

Her eyes were fixed on him, and a faint wave of color crept up into her face. "I never saw you here before."

"I just bought this store this morning. I was trying to straighten it out."

Distaste touched her face. "Whatever you do will be an improvement. I never came in here unless I was forced to."

Steve smiled at her. "I imagine a lot of customers must have felt that way. Lewis seemed pretty anxious to sell."

"He should have," she sniffed. "He was losing money."

So many little mannerisms reminded him of Sally. Sally was forthright and direct. She didn't hesitate to say what was on her mind.

"I'm Steve Truman," he ventured.

She extended a hand. "I know. I've seen you around town. People pointed you out."

Steve glowed inwardly. She must have been impressed to ask people about him.

A small frown was settling on her face. "But you were a deputy then."

He couldn't help but feel his spirits sinking. Was a deputy's job more important to her? "I was," he said steadily. "I resigned last night. I got tired of shooting at people and being shot at in return. So I bought this store."

Her smile returned. "Now you can live a normal life. It must be horrible for a wife to know that her man is always in danger."

"I'm not married," Steve said, his lip corners twitching. He knew what she was doing.

Her eyes crinkled, and white teeth flashed. "That's what I wanted to know," she said with satisfaction.

Steve threw back his head and roared with laughter. She might be a little minx, but she would never be dull. "How do I learn your name?"

She cut her eyes at him. "Asking is the most direct way. I'm Linda Martin."

"Are you always so direct, Linda?"

She wrinkled her nose at him. "Usually. I find it saves so much time."

This girl was going to be a delight to know. Steve's heart picked up an irregular beat. Daniels had said something about getting a good woman back of him. Had he already found her?

"I'd better get what I came for," she said, "or Pa will strip off my hide."

"I'd sure hate for that to happen," Steve said and grinned. "What can I get for you?"

"Pa's building a shed, and he ran out of nails. He wants No. 8 nails." At Steve's consternation, she frowned. "Don't tell me you're out of them."

"I'm sure they're around here someplace," Steve said frantically. He couldn't lose the most important customer he would ever have. He waved a hand at the interior of the store. "They've got to be in here somewhere." A brazen streak of audacity seized him. "Maybe you'd help me look. The next time you come in, I promise I'll have this store in some kind of order."

"What would the nails be in?"

Steve scowled unhappily, remembering Lewis' carelessness. "They should be in a keg, but knowing Lewis he could have put them anywhere."

"Maybe I should go to another store," she said in indecision.

"Please don't," he begged. "We'll look for ten minutes. If we don't find them by then, we'll give up."

That impish little smile worked at her lip corners. "It'll do Pa good to rest a little bit. Show me where to start."

Linda found the first keg, tucked into a gloomy corner. She picked a nail out of the keg and held it up. "This looks smaller than the ones he's been using."

Steve wasn't sure of his nail sizes. He bent over to peer at the label on the keg. He straightened, shaking his head. "No; these are No. 4s."

"Doesn't that disappoint you?" How her eyes shone.

He was bolder than he had ever been in his life. "No," he said. "If they were the right size, you'd be gone too soon." He caught his breath. Maybe that would offend her.

"You," she said with asperity, but the shine didn't dim in her eyes.

Lewis ran the damnedest store Steve had ever seen. He was beginning to believe there were no No. 8s when he spotted another keg. He hurried to it, saying, "This has to be it." He pulled out a nail before he looked at the label on the keg. It seemed the right size. No. 8 was the most common nail used. The tag confirmed his opinion. "Yes, this is it. How many do you want?"

"Pa says about ten pounds."

Steve was beginning to sweat before he found a supply of sacks. She must believe he was the most inefficient man who ever lived. Now he had to find the scales. They shouldn't be hard to spot.

He measured out ten pounds of nails, then slid them into a paper sack. She stood near him all the time he was weighing and packaging the nails. He was very aware of her presence. Her perfume was so sweet-smelling he thought it would make him giddy. He folded the sack down and wrapped several strands of string around it. Oh Lord, if he could only think of something to hold her here a little longer.

He hefted the package in his hand. "That's going to be pretty heavy for you. Perhaps I should carry it home for you."

Her dancing eyes mocked him. Steve felt the color rising in his cheeks. She knew what he was trying to do. She took the package from his hand. "You think I'm too weak to carry this?"

"No," he said frantically, his flush increasing. "It's just—" The words clogged in his throat.

"It's just that you don't want me to go," she finished for him.

He blew out a gusty breath. She had a directness that again reminded him so much of Sally. "Yes," he admitted. "I didn't know how to say it."

Her eyes still danced despite the sternness of her face. "I've always found it best to come right out and say what's on your mind."

He tried to look contrite and couldn't. That would be a form of deceit, and she had already proven she didn't like that. He grinned and said, "I was thinking of some way to hold you. I was afraid I wouldn't see you again."

Her laughter rang out gay and lilting. "That's better. I'll be back tomorrow."

"That's a promise?"

"I said so, didn't I? I've learned that when a man's building something, he constantly runs out of one thing or another. If Pa doesn't, I'll hide one of his tools."

He wanted to reach out and grasp her hands, but that

would be pushing things a little fast. "You're merely wonderful," he said gravely.

That brought color to her face. "You're not so bad, either."

Steve watched her leave the store, the coins she had given him for the nails clutched in his hand. He didn't think he'd ever spend those coins.

Jimmy came up and broke his trance by saying, "You're kinda gone on her, aren't you?"

Steve ducked his head. "You don't know a damned thing about it."

"Only what I can see," Jimmy jeered. "I don't blame you. She's a looker."

Steve draped an arm across the boy's shoulders. "You see too much for your own good. Jimmy, I think we're going to get along just fine."

CHAPTER 25

CLEATIS kept a block behind Steve as he followed him down the street. Cleatis had followed him a half-dozen times and had added to his store of knowledge about him. The night he missed Steve still rankled, but now he had enough additional information to make his next attempt a sure thing.

Cleatis had learned that Steve had handed in his badge. That wouldn't do him any good. He wasn't going to escape Cleatis' vengeance. Steve had killed or was responsible for the killing of both of his brothers, and by God, he was going to pay for that.

Every time Cleatis thought about those killings, he trembled. Just give him one more chance, and he would wipe out the necessity of carrying this hatred with him.

He followed Steve back to the hardware store and nodded in satisfaction. Steve would work late tonight; he usually did. Maybe tonight would be the time. Cleatis felt that peculiar itching of his palms. They always itched when he was so keyed up. He stopped across the street and watched Steve enter the store. A big, new sign covered most of the window. The sign read, "Opened under new management."

Cleatis scratched his right palm. The store was doing a great business, but Steve wasn't going to live long enough to enjoy it.

Cleatis watched the store patiently. Steve would be amazed to know how much Cleatis knew about him. Cleatis had seen that good-looking woman come in and out of the store a dozen times. She and the ex-deputy were pretty cozy. They walked together arm in arm, their heads close together. Twice he had seen Steve brush her cheek with a kiss. Something was growing between them, but that, like the store's business, wasn't going to do Steve any good.

Cleatis turned and walked back to the stable. Jorman gave him ample time off, but he was always careful to work longer hours to make up for it. He wanted this bothersome job done; he wanted to go home and tell Linus of his success.

Cleatis had thought briefly of killing the woman. He was sure Steve would mourn over that. But he had discarded the idea quickly. The woman hadn't done the Divens any harm. Killing her wouldn't rub away his insatiable thirst for Steve's blood.

Tonight, he thought, and nodded in hardening determination. He could come back to the hardware store and follow Steve when he left for the night. All those hours of shadowing his quarry had laid out a pattern. If the pattern held true, Steve would walk over to the woman's house. That route was an ideal place for an ambush. The house lay out of the business district, and the street leading to it was dark.

He walked up to Jorman. Jorman was sitting in his favorite chair in the runway. He spent most of his time there. Cleatis wondered how the chair managed to hold up under such abuse.

"Mr. Jorman," he said hesitantly, "I'd like to go out again tonight."

Jorman managed to keep the annoyance off his face.

This man was too good to lose. He couldn't afford to rile him.

"You're going out often, Cleatis," petulance showing in his voice.

Cleatis looked at the ground. "I always try to make it up."

"You do," Jorman said quickly. "I hope it's not some woman who's got her hooks into you."

"No woman," Cleatis denied. "I'll be back just as soon as I can. After tonight, I won't ask for any more time off."

The severity of Jorman's face eased. "That'll be all right." His eyelids were beginning to droop.

Cleatis busied himself with a few odd tasks. If the past was any indication, it would be several hours before Steve left his store. Cleatis could slip in the tackroom shortly before he thought Steve was due to leave. He could stick the rifle down his overall leg and go out the back entrance. He doubted Jorman would even know he was gone.

Cleatis was across the street only a few minutes before Steve came out. He wasn't working as late as usual. Cleatis watched him close and lock the door behind him.

Good, he thought savagely. He could get this over earlier than he hoped.

He stayed a good distance behind Steve, walking a little stiff-legged because of the rifle barrel. He wasn't fearful of losing Steve. Experience had taught him where Steve would go.

The talk, the laughter, and the noise of the business district fell behind him. Not once did Steve look behind him. Cleatis smiled bleakly. Steve was too absorbed in where he was going to even think of looking back.

The street was dark, but there was enough moonlight to see. Cleatis silently closed the distance between them. He had already picked the spot from which he would shoot. That big, gnarled elm tree would be excellent, and it wouldn't be too long a shot.

Steve would have to cross the street a few yards down to get to the girl's house. At this time of night, traffic along this street was rare. Pure chance had saved Steve on the first attempt. It would not happen again.

Cleatis eased in behind the elm and, after taking the rifle from his overalls, peered across the street. Steve was almost halfway across. Cleatis' finger tensed on the trigger.

He would give him another step before blasting him to hell.

Steve's heart sang a little refrain. His head was filled with the thoughts of seeing Linda again. It was odd how Daniels' remark about finding a good woman to back him stuck with him. He had found Linda; his quest was over.

The hard pound of running hoofs suddenly filled the quiet night air. Steve's head jerked sharply to his left. He saw two horses racing toward him, their riders bent over their backs, their mouths stretched wide with their yelling. Steve could guess at what was happening. Two drunken cowboys were out on a lark, using this quiet street as a racetrack.

He was caught in the middle of the street. He couldn't cross it before one or both of those horses were on him. He yelled an oath at the top of his lungs. Either the riders didn't hear him, or were too drunk to care.

Steve left his feet in a long, desperate dive. He threw himself into the air and heard the nasty little whine of a rifle bullet. It could have been imagination, but he thought he felt the air of its passage. The second time flashed through his mind as he landed on one shoulder. He curled up and rolled. He did not attempt to slow his momentum. He remembered the first attempt on his life vividly. His skin tingled in anticipation of another shot. He came to a stop and spat dust out of his mouth. He had slammed into the ground pretty hard, and it left his head spinning and dizzy. He scrambled around in time to see a dark shadow leave the big elm tree and run off into the darkness. Even if he had hopes of catching him, Steve had no desire to pursue him unarmed. Steve stood and brushed himself off, not surprised to find that his hands were shaking. He had better tell Linda what had happened, then report this second attempt to Daniels.

Linda answered his knock, the joy fading from her eyes as she saw his disheveled, dusty appearance. "Steve, what happened?" she gasped.

"Somebody took a shot at me," he said grimly. "I've got to report it to Marshal Daniels."

She tried to detain him. "Do you think it wise to be out now? Whoever it was could try again."

Steve impatiently shook his head. "I don't think so. I caught a glimpse of him running away." He anticipated her next question and shook his head. "No, I didn't recognize him." He bent and kissed her forehead. "Get that worried look off your face. I'll be all right. I'll be back after I talk to Daniels."

Daniels sat across the desk his head canted attentively as he listened to Steve's words. "You didn't get a chance of a shot at him?"

"I wasn't carrying a gun," Steve said shortly.

"You think he was waiting for you?"

"I sure do. I didn't see anybody following me. He was behind that big elm almost directly across the street from the Martins' house." Daniels' frown made him realize that Daniels didn't know what he was talking about. "I was on my way to see Linda Martin, the girl I've been seeing."

"And this one was waiting for you?"

"Yes," Steve said flatly.

"Turning in your badge evidently didn't wipe away somebody's hatred," Daniels mused. "And he knows enough about you to know your movements."

Steve shivered. He had come to the same conclusion himself. Not now, he wailed silently. Now that I've found Linda.

"Do you have any idea who it could be?" Daniels asked.

"I've racked my brain," Steve said dully. "I haven't come up with a thing."

"You'd better start packing a gun," Daniels advised. "Change your pattern. Don't do anything the same way. Maybe we can mix him up. We'll look over that ground in the morning."

Steve nodded wearily. God, this incident had left him more beaten than prolonged physical activity. "I'll be here in the morning, Dan." He stood and took a couple of steps toward the door, then stopped. "I think I know what we'll find. One spent rifle shell."

"The same as the first time?"

Steve nodded. "A shot from a single-shot rifle. That's the only explanation I can think of to explain why he doesn't shoot a second time." He was so tight inwardly that he hurt. Twice the unknown attacker had him helpless and hadn't taken advantage of it. "This makes me feel so damned helpless, Dan."

He nodded jerkily and left the office.

CHAPTER 26

FRUSTRATION was eating Cleatis alive. He had failed two times, and it was bothering his sleep. Every time he closed his eyes, he could see Linus staring reproachfully at him. "You failed me, son." The words had a mournful ring.

"It wasn't my fault, Pa," Cleatis protested. "I had him dead in my sights, and both times a freak accident saved him. Next time, I won't miss."

But there might not be a next time. Steve had completely changed his routine. He changed his time of arrival at the store; a couple of times, he had stayed the whole night there. Sometimes he used the rear door, for Cleatis had seen him enter the store, then not reappear at all.

It was confusing, if not downright scary. The more Cleatis thought about it, the more worried he became. He couldn't explain why, but things seemed to have changed. Instead of him feeling he was hunting Steve down, the roles had been switched. Steve was now hunting him.

Worse, Jorman was no longer as sympathetic as he had been. He didn't give Cleatis all the time off he needed. Cleatis could no longer watch Steve as closely as he wanted. Oh he could quit his job and watch Steve to his heart's content. But he needed the job to pay for his food. All he wanted was one more crack at Steve, then he could quit this damned job and go home. He thought of how Linus would look if he returned home a failure. He couldn't bear the thought of those reproachful eyes laying that heavy load on him.

The answer to his problem came clear and shining. Instead of him going after Steve, make Steve come to him. How could he do that? That was easy. Use the woman. He had to get out again tonight. Jorman might be unhappy about it, but Cleatis didn't care.

He approached Jorman, who was sitting as usual in his chair. "Boss, I'm going out for supper now. I might be gone a little longer than usual."

Jorman's lips compressed in a thin, tight line. This was happening far too often. Jorman could put his foot down, but that could mean he would lose Cleatis' services. Every time Jorman thought of Cleatis' willingness, all thoughts of rebuking him faded. Cleatis had a woman; Jorman was certain of that. If he only held his patience, all this would fade away. Cleatis was young. Real or simulated love was only a phase he was going through.

"All right, Cleatis," Jorman said petulantly. "Get back as soon as you can."

"I will," Cleatis replied. He wasn't sure he would be back at all. It all depended upon how this night turned out. If he succeeded in killing Steve, he would leave for home.

He walked into the tackroom and thrust the rifle down his overall leg. Just the thought of what was ahead made his palms sweat. What if the woman didn't come out? What if Steve visited her house instead? Cleatis' nerves felt tight at the thought of Steve catching him while he was trying to kidnap the woman. All hell would break loose. But if a man was going to succeed, he had to gamble a little.

It was dark by the time he reached the big elm tree across from the woman's house. He didn't know how long he would have to wait. He writhed at the prospects of her not coming out at all.

He had already chosen a place to take her. That old Grimes farmhouse just outside of town. It had been abandoned years ago, and no one ever visited the old ruin. It would be an ideal place to hold her, using her as bait to draw Steve. Cleatis had everything in readiness. He had cloth and rope in his pocket. Everything depended upon getting her away from her house.

Time dragged away. Jorman would be outraged at his prolonged absence. Cleatis had laid out his plan, and he had to follow it. Steve's appearance here was the only thing that would make him abandon it. He shifted his weight. He had the dogged patience of an animal. His eyes never left the door of the house across the street.

A soft little sigh escaped him as he saw the door open. A woman's form was silhouetted in the doorway, then the door closed behind her. Cleatis had no idea where she was going. It made no difference. He could pick her up before she got a block away from her house.

He fell into step behind her, quickly closing the intervening distance. He came up behind her silently, and the muzzle of the rifle jabbed into her back before she was aware of his presence.

"You scream, and I'll shoot," he growled.

A little squeak of terror escaped her. "Who are you?" she gasped. "What do you want?"

Cleatis jabbed her with the rifle muzzle. "Just keep on walking and keep your mouth shut." Another jab emphasized his words. After he had finished with Steve, the problem remained of what to do with the woman. Turn her loose, or leave her there in the old farmhouse? He didn't know what the answer would be. He hadn't figured that far ahead.

Prods of the rifle muzzle kept her guided in the right direction. She didn't dare resist the threat of the rifle, but she tried to talk to him. "I don't know you. Who are you? Where are you taking me?"

Cleatis remained stubbornly silent. He avoided the lighted streets and the crowded areas. If anybody tried to approach too close, he steered her in a different direction. Twice, he saw a tensing in her figure at a person's approach, and he hissed, "If you call out, I'll shoot you right here. I mean it. Just do as you're told, and you won't be hurt. Obey me, and all this will soon be over." The slumping of her shoulders told him she was accepting his warning.

His face was alit when they were less than a half mile from the old Grimes house. He was going to make it. He had audaciously kidnaped her almost out of the heart of Oklahoma City, and nobody was the wiser. Perhaps this was a sign, telling him the rest of the night would be just as successful.

Fear touched Linda's face, and she tried to hold back when they came up to the old ruin of a house. Cleatis prodded her forward. "Go on in," he growled.

"I won't," she said frantically. "You can't make me. You—"

He lifted the rifle barrel and brought it down in a short, chopping blow. It caught her across the back of the head. A hollow groan escaped her, her knees buckled, and she slumped to the ground. He picked her up and carried her inside the building. He hadn't wanted to do that, but she had left him no other course. He bent low over the still, white face. She was still breathing. She might have a headache, but otherwise she would be all right.

"I didn't want to do that," he muttered. "You just threw in with the wrong man. Don't you see, I had to use you to bring him here."

Cleatis bound Linda's hands and feet securely, then stuffed a gag into her mouth. She might recover consciousness before he returned, and he couldn't take the risk of her screams being heard. He tested the bonds before he straightened. Her breathing was regular, though a little shallow. Now he had to put the final touches on this little plan.

Outside, he stopped and looked all around him. The night was still, and there were no alarming sounds.

He hurried back to town. He had to figure some way to get a message to Steve, the message that would draw him out to the Grimes house.

When he got into town, Cleatis went into a restaurant and ordered coffee. He labored over a short note. His hands weren't even shaking. Tonight, he couldn't miss.

He paid for the coffee and walked outside. He hadn't figured out yet how he was going to get the note to Steve, but the way his luck was running, something would occur to him.

His eyes lit up with an unholy joy as he saw the boy coming down the street toward him. He knew the boy; he had seen him coming and leaving Steve's hardware store. "Hold up a minute, boy," he said harshly.

The boy stopped, his figure going tense. To the best of his knowledge, he had never seen this man before.

"Do you know Steve Truman?"

"I work for him," Jimmy said proudly.

"Good. Give this note to him." Cleatis handed over the folded piece of paper. "Make it right away. It's important." He spun and quickened his pace.

"Wait a minute," Jimmy called after him. "What's your name?"

The big figure never slackened his stride.

Jimmy shook his head. The whole thing was odd. He'd better get this note to Steve as fast as he could.

CHAPTER 27

JIMMY handed Steve the note. "Some big guy told me to give this to you. He said it was important."

Steve's face went white as he read the note, and his jaws clenched. The crudely scrawled note read, "If you want to see your woman again, you'd better get out to the Grimes house." His eyes were wild as he glanced at Jimmy. "Who gave you this?"

Jimmy shook his head. "Never saw him before. He was a big man dressed in overalls."

A thousand questions crowded up to Steve's tongue. He wanted to ask which way he went, and where he came from. None of those questions were important now. The only important thing was that Linda was being held at the old Grimes house.

He took the belt wrapped gun out of a drawer. He didn't know why, but the feeling of security it gave him wasn't important, either. Linda could be in real danger. He buckled on the belt, lifted the gun from its holster, then let it slide back. He had the dreadful feeling that he was going to need his former dexterity more than ever before.

Jimmy watched him, big-eyed. "Are you figuring on trouble?"

"I don't know what's ahead of me," Steve said brusquely. "Keep an eye on the store until I get back."

He left the store at a run, slowing after a dozen paces. He wasn't going to rush out to the Grimes place without knowing for sure that Linda was gone. He changed direction and picked up his pace. Linda might still be home. He could check that with her father.

He pounded on the Martin door. He thought Mr. Martin would never answer.

Mr. Martin showed surprise at the sight of Steve. "What are you doing here? Did you pass Linda?"

Steve's throat went dry and tight. "Did she go out?"

"She went to your store. Left about an hour ago."

There wasn't any use alarming Linda's father, not until Steve knew for sure. His fear was mounting, beating on his nerves like a great drumstick. Steve didn't know why, but some crazy man had abducted Linda.

"I missed her, Mr. Martin. I'd better go back and see if I can find her."

"Come in and have a beer," Mr. Martin offered.

Steve shook his head. He and Mr. Martin had a good relationship, and he certainly didn't want to destroy it by turning down an invitation. He smiled and shrugged. "I'd like nothing better, Mr. Martin. I musta got her instructions mixed up. I don't want to keep Linda waiting. You know how women are."

Mr. Martin smiled in sympathy. "Know what you're up against, son. A man has to keep a woman pacified, or she can get out of sorts pretty easy. Come back with her. We can have that beer then."

"Looking forward to it," Steve said easily. He sauntered casually down the street. The moment he was sure he was out of sight of the house he broke into a hard run.

He ran until he was breathless, then slowed until he could catch his breath. He knew where the old Grimes place was. It was rapidly settling into total ruin. But why had this crazy man taken Linda there? Steve choked back an oath. He wouldn't have any answers until he got there and found out for himself.

The ghostly bulk of the old building rose a couple of hundred yards ahead of him. It wasn't a brilliant night, for the moon scudded across a cloudy sky. Steve stopped and stared at the ramshackle house. Was the kidnaper expecting him to walk straight up to that house?

Steve's lips thinned. The man was using Linda as bait to draw him close. But how had he found out about Linda? Steve couldn't answer that, either. Was this the same man who had shot at him twice? Everything suddenly jelled and became clearer. The former failures had made this man more cautious. The man knew enough about Steve to be aware that Linda had become an integral part of his life. The miserable bastard, using her like this.

But this was no time to lose his head. Uncontrollable

rage would push him right into those waiting hands. He couldn't take a step unless some sane thinking was behind it. He cocked an eye at the sky and nodded at a moving patch of cloud. Now was the time to take advantage of the obscurity it would give him.

He moved a cautious step at a time. Motion was the greatest betrayer of all life, man and animal. Steve was hunkered down when the moon appeared again. He could feel the thin film of sweat break out on his body. It made a man feel crawly to think that hostile eyes could be watching every step he took.

Steve judged the movement of the clouds and moved only when the moon disappeared again. He didn't know how long it took him to reach the house, but it seemed forever. Not a single hostile move had been made against him; maybe this whole thing was some cruel hoax.

It would be unwise to try to go in through the front door. No, by keeping close to the house, he would work his way around to the back.

He kept a firm control on his nerves. He wouldn't let an unwise movement betray him. He discarded the rear door for the same reason as the front: the possibility of being expected to use it. But there were plenty of entrances to this old house. The last three windows he had passed were knocked out.

The moon came out full again, and Steve risked a quick glimpse through one of the glassless windows. He almost choked in rage, and barely managed to stop himself from climbing directly through the window. The light was strong enough for Steve to catch a glimpse of Linda. She was bound to one of the supporting posts, and while he couldn't plainly see her face, he thought a cloth was tied around her mouth.

He stared briefly at her, his eyes burning. She had known terror and indignity at this handling. Steve had never known such a killing rage. He wanted to rush to her, but he restrained himself. He glanced slowly around the big room. He didn't see the man responsible for this outrage, but Steve had no doubt he was somewhere around. He climbed through the window frame, holding back an oath as a shard of glass bit at his knee. The small sting wasn't bad enough to take his mind off his major objective.

Cleatis finished tying Linda firmly to the upright support in the main room. "I hate to do this, ma'am," he said. "But you'd yell to him when you see him coming." He placed a folded piece of cloth across her mouth and knotted it securely behind her head.

"Try to yell all you want to now," he said with frosty humor. He walked across the room and stepped into a small closet. The door wouldn't close, but it didn't matter. That small crack would give him a wide enough view.

He saw Linda staring frantically at him above the gag before he pulled the door shut as far as it would go. He didn't know what he was going to do with the woman. Maybe he would just let her go after he killed Steve. He would be long gone from Oklahoma City before she alerted the authorities.

He sank down and rested on his heels. This closet didn't give him much room. He banged into the walls every way he turned. It was going to be an uncomfortable wait, but it shouldn't last too long. He hadn't seen a sign of Steve, and that caused him a little concern. But Steve would come. Cleatis knew that with a deep conviction. He had seen how much this woman meant to Steve.

What the hell was that woman doing? She kept ducking and bobbing her head. Then Cleatis realized what she was trying to do: She was trying to free herself. The effort wouldn't do her any good. He had checked every knot. They'd hold as long as he wanted them to.

His head swung back as he thought he heard a sound. Something was moving at the far end of the room. The moon had gone under the clouds, and he couldn't clearly make out what it was. A savage exultation flooded him as the figure came nearer. The bait had worked well. Truman was in the house.

Cleatis picked up the rifle. He had it cocked and ready as he pushed open the door.

"Steve!" a scream rang out. "Watch out! He's in the closet!"

Steve drew his pistol as he clambered into the room. He took a cautious step at a time, trying to avoid the treacherous creak of a board. He could see Linda plainly. She was bobbing and weaving her head, and he wondered what she was trying to do. Then he knew! She was trying to free the gag from her mouth. He ached for the misery it caused her. He wished he could call to her to wait, but he didn't dare risk calling out.

He froze as he heard Linda scream. "Steve! Watch out! He's in the closet."

Steve saw the closet door open, and his pistol swung around to cover the door.

Cleatis, in his eagerness to be free of the confines of the closet, didn't judge his space correctly. He swung the rifle's muzzle too quickly, and it banged against the doorjamb. He cursed as he fought to correct his mistake; then he was clear of the closet, and the muzzle was swinging up.

Steve's pistol lanced out flame, and a tremendous force hit Cleatis just below the breastbone. He fought to keep his hold on the rifle, but all the strength was flowing out of his hands and legs. He dropped the rifle and tried to stay erect, but his legs had gone suddenly weak. He thought he was screaming, but no sound came. After all this effort, he had failed. He fell heavily to the floor.

Steve advanced cautiously to him. The rifle lay less than a yard from the big figure, and Steve kicked it farther away.

That should take care of all the weapons, but Steve didn't throw caution to the winds. He moved with elaborate care as he bent over the figure.

He thought the man was dead; then he saw a weak fluttering of the eyelids. The man stared up at him, and there was no mistaking the hatred in the eyes.

"Goddamn you," Cleatis said feebly.

Steve squatted down beside him. This man was going fast. "Why?" Steve asked in wonder.

"You killed my brothers." Cleatis stopped and choked, and blood gushed from his mouth. "You killed Charley and Elmer. Pa wanted me to get you in payment."

"Are you a Divens?"

"I'm a Divens," Cleatis replied. His mouth sagged open, and his eyes went blank and unseeing.

Steve straightened wearily and walked over to Linda. The Divens were apparently a bloodthirsty clan. Were there more of them? Would the evil head of this family send somebody else after him?

He pulled a knife from his pocket, opened a blade and severed the bonds holding Linda. She fell into his arms, crying softly. "Oh Steve. I was so frightened."

He patted her shoulder. "Easy, easy. It's all over now, Linda."

"I knew he was going to try to kill you." She blinked back the tears. She was making every effort to keep from going to pieces. "I didn't think I could warn you. I kept working at that gag with my tongue. It finally slipped enough so that I could call out to you."

"Come on. I'm going to take you home," Steve said woodenly. He realized what this moment could mean. They had gone through a mutual danger, and it had removed customary restrictions. She was soft and giving, but he couldn't take advantage. Knowing him had gotten her into serious trouble. He could not let her go through that again.

Linda kept giving him troubled glances as they walked. Something had erected a barrier between them. She didn't know what it was, but the longer she faced it, the more reserved she grew.

Steve left her at the door of her house. "I'll see you one of these days, Linda," he said in a frozen voice.

She stared after his retreating figure. She didn't know why this was happening, but he had plainly changed his mind about her. The tears slowly trickled down her cheeks.

CHAPTER 28

STEVE returned to the marshal's office with Daniels. Together they had brought Cleatis in and left him with Andrews.

"Go over it once again, Steve," Daniels said. He listened attentively as Steve related how he had received the note and hurried out to the old Grimes house.

"He had her, all right," he said in a tired voice. "I managed to slip into the house. She worked the gag out of her mouth and screamed a warning to me. I whirled in time. He was trying to bring a rifle up on me. The same rifle he used twice before."

Daniels shook his head. "A plumb crazy man."

"Not by his reasoning, Dan. I killed and brought in one of his brothers while I was a deputy. His other brother was killed at about the same time. He blamed me for both their deaths."

"Did you find out who he is?"

"He said he was a Divens. His pa sent him out here to avenge the death of Charley and Elmer."

"It's no loss," Daniels said callously. "This oughta bring you closer to the Martin girl."

"Or push us farther apart," Steve said hollowly. "I don't dare attempt to see her again. I don't know how many of the Divens there are left. If their old man tried it once, he could try it again. I couldn't put her through all this again."

"Divens, Divens," Daniels mused. "Where are they from?"

Steve wearily shook his head. "I haven't the slightest idea. This ought to be all over, and I feel as tight as ever."

"I talked to Jorman about losing his man. I tell you he was shocked. He didn't know where he came from, either, though he had the feeling it might have been from Arkansas. He said this man had the Arkansas twang, and he dressed that way."

His eyes were beginning to shine. "My former district was in Arkansas. I used to know a Cal Duncan. He was a sheriff out of Harrison. A damned good, hard-nosed man. He kept on top of things. I'll wire him and see what he knows about the Divens. You just sit tight until I hear from Duncan."

Steve nodded despondently. He didn't think much would come of it.

A week passed, then two. Steve didn't ask Daniels if he had received a reply to his wire. He didn't think it mattered anyway. Three times during those weeks, he had passed Linda on the street. Twice, he had tried to talk to her. She flushed, and her lips were tightly compressed. Her eyes never did warm up. There was no way he could explain to her that he was only trying to protect her. He had erected this barrier solely for her safety.

The third time she passed him by, looking straight ahead as though he didn't exist.

Cal Duncan muttered lurid oaths as he read the long telegram from Oklahoma City. He wasn't surprised that a bad end had come to Charley and Elmer. Linus had never kept any control on those boys, and they had grown up wild. He was surprised they hadn't gotten in serious trouble around here. But Cleatis was a different matter. A poor, dumb, hard-working kid without a mean bone in his body. His only serious flaw was that he blindly obeyed his father. So Linus had gotten him killed.

Linus saw the horseman coming, and until he got much closer, he didn't recognize who it was. Then his lips pressed together in a tight, bloodless line. He was always uncomfortable when a lawman was around. What the hell could Duncan want out this way?

Linus put a false smile on his face as Duncan pulled up before the porch. "Howdy, Cal. I'd get up, but this here leg is paining me something awful." He squirmed uneasily. Cal Duncan had the coldest pair of eyes he'd ever seen.

Duncan remained silent for so long that Linus' discomfort grew. "Did you ride out here just to stare at me, Cal?" he complained.

"Maybe you've hit on it, Linus. I've been trying to figure out what kind of a father you are."

Linus could feel his cheeks burn, and he couldn't tell why. "What's that supposed to mean?" He tried to sound angry, but there was a false note in his tone.

"So you finally got Cleatis killed. You might just as well have pulled the trigger yourself."

Linus' mouth flew open. He felt as though he had been kicked in the stomach. "Cleatis?" he babbled. "I don't know what you mean." For some cruel reason, Duncan was trying to scare him.

"Oh you know, all right. You sent Cleatis to Oklahoma City to kill Steve Truman. Steve was only doing his job when he brought Elmer in. Charley got himself killed. He earned it."

That jolted a flash of resentment from Linus. "Both of them were good boys. That Truman and Dixon deserved killing."

"So Cleatis was the one who killed Sam," Duncan observed. "Dixon was a good man. Why, goddamn you! I ought to haul you in for setting this thing in motion. Charley and Elmer were both worthless, cheap criminals. They were waiting trial for a couple of murders when they broke jail. They killed three more before they got away."

"No!" Linus screamed. "I won't believe that. They were good boys. They even sent me money several times."

"Money they got from their crimes," Duncan lashed out. "I don't know how you talked Cleatis into going after Sam and Steve, but it got him killed."

The enormity of this moment finally sank in, leaving Linus dazed and sick. Cleatis was dead. All his boys were gone. He was completely alone. What was he going to do? "Cal, I'm all alone now." The words were a little, animal-like moan.

Duncan shook his head in disgust. "You really didn't think Cleatis could have gotten away with it, did you? He wasn't bright enough to start with."

Linus held his head in his hands and rocked back and forth. "What am I going to do now?"

There was no pity in Duncan's face. He stabbed a fore-finger at Linus. "I'll tell you what you're going to do: You're going to pray that nothing happens to Steve. You better pray that he lives a long and peaceful life. If anything happens to him, I'm coming after you. I'm going to put a charge against you of inciting murder. If you think it won't stick, you just wait and see."

Linus shrank back into his chair. "You can't do that," he squalled in pure terror.

"Try me," Duncan snapped. "I wish there was something I could do now. Cleatis was a good kid even if he was a little on the dumb side."

Tears were pouring out of Linus' eyes. "I ain't going to make a move against Truman."

"You better not even think about it," Duncan said sternly. His eyes bored into the groveling wreck. "Worthless old bastard," he growled and wheeled his horse around.

Linus couldn't see very well. His eyes were too filled with tears. This was a heartless world. Nobody gave a damn what happened to him.

Daniels walked to the door and hailed Steve. "Come in here. I want to talk to you."

Steve walked listlessly into Daniels' office. "You didn't hear from your wire," Steve stated.

"For a bright young man you sure guess wrong a lot," Daniels said cheerfully. "Just heard from Duncan this morning." He waited until Steve sat down. "Don't you want to hear what he says?"

"There are more Divens," Steve said, his voice dull.

"Just one. A sick old man. Even if he was capable of trying for you again, he couldn't. Duncan hobbled him real good. Old Divens will be scared to even turn his head."

Steve was too slow in comprehending what Daniels said, so slow that it irritated Daniels.

"Don't you hear what I'm saying? I know you've been avoiding that girl in some crazy notion of protecting her. Don't you understand? You're free to go after her. Nothing should have stopped you from the first."

The joy flooding back into Steve's face was something to see. He came alive, and his eyes sparkled. "Dan," he babbled, "is this all true? I don't know how to thank you."

"You can believe it," Daniels said solemnly. "Don't waste your time hanging around here talking to me. Get after her. I hope for your sake you're not too late. Now get out of here. I've got work to do." He shook his head as Steve bounded out of the office. There went a lucky young man. He had a good future ahead of him.

Steve didn't run on the way to the Martins' house, but he came as close as he could without breaking into a wild dash. He slowed as he came in sight of the house. What was he going to say to Linda? His heart was beating fast and hard as he knocked on the door. Oh God, let her listen to him.

Mr. Martin answered the knock. "You! You got a lot of nerve coming here."

"It's all right, Mr. Martin," Steve said huskily. "Is Linda here?"

"She doesn't want to see you," Mr. Martin growled.

Steve pushed by him. He wasn't going to waste time trying to explain to Linda's father. The only important thing was that Linda listen to him.

Linda was just coming into the room, and she stopped, one hand going to her throat at the sight of him.

"Linda." He reached for her hands.

She evaded his grasp, and her eyes were resentful. But Steve thought he detected mute begging in them.

Mr. Martin came up behind him. "Haven't you bothered her enough?" he asked tartly.

Steve ignored him. "Linda, listen to me. I was afraid there might be more Divens coming after me. The man who kidnaped you was Cleatis Divens. When I was deputy marshal, I killed one of his brothers. He came after me to even the score. I couldn't risk you being harmed again. Now I know it's all over, Linda. The only Divens left is a sick old man. Don't you understand what I'm saying? It's all over."

The stony façade of her face was melting. She wanted to believe him.

"Linda, do you think I wanted to stay away from you? I thought I would die a little more with each passing day. Just when things looked their brightest, that big hulk came along. Linda, the business is doing better than I ever hoped for. All it needs to make everything worthwhile is you."

He turned in desperation to her father. "Mr. Martin, do you understand what I'm trying to say? I'm trying to ask her to marry me."

A broad, forgiving grin spread across Martin's face. "I think I do now. Answer him, Linda."

She looked coolly at Steve. In his anxiety he didn't see the ghost of a smile forming on her lips. "I'd have to give that some serious thought, Steve."

He waited for what seemed an aeon. Then a radiant smile spread across her face. "I've thought about it long enough. Oh yes, Steve!"

She came into his arms, and he didn't care who was watching. He kissed her, and her response was more than ample.

Mr. Martin tugged on his arm. "Hey, how about that beer now? You didn't come back for the one I offered you before."

Steve sighed. Mr. Martin picked the damnedest times to intrude. But Steve guessed he'd better accept the offer now. It wouldn't be wise to offend his future father-in-law twice in a row.

Books
for those who
feel deeply about
wild unsettled places

NE-11

Ballantine brings you the best of the West— And the best western authors